I0575805

The Miracle Girl

THE MIRACLE GIRL

James Upsilon

Copyright © 2024 by James Upsilon

All rights reserved
ISBN 979-8-9924995-2-0

Independently Published

This book is sold subject to the condition that it shall not,
by way of trade or otherwise, be lent, resold, hired out, or
otherwise circulated in any form of binding or cover
other than that in which it is published without the
publisher's prior consent and without a similar condition,
including this condition, being imposed on the
subsequent purchaser.

To Anna and Hayden, my first readers

CONTENTS

Author's Note:

This novel includes depictions of mental illness. I have attempted to portray these situations accurately from my experience as a licensed therapist. However, individual experience with mental health varies so widely that it is impossible to capture every possibility in a single narrative. If you have a friend or family member who struggles with mental health challenges, trust their description of their experience over the one conveyed in this work.

Chapter 1

Micah slams the latest issue of the *Squatch Watch* onto the desk in front of me, making me jump. I glance up at him, bracing myself for what I already know is coming.

"Why does your junk keep getting left on the couch like this?"

"Well..."

"Should I just throw it in the garbage next time? That's where it belongs anyway."

Anger flares up inside of me, but I shove the feeling away. The snide comment isn't actually what I'm worried about. It's what's coming next.

"If you can give me one shred of evidence that Sasquatch is anything more than a demented fairy tale, I'll stop bothering you about it."

The snarky smirk on his face turns my stomach. I am *so tired* of him turning every other conversation into some kind of philosophical dissertation.

"I've told you, I don't believe in all of that."

"Why do you keep it around then?" His eyes gleam as he turns the screws tighter.

"What do you care?" I snap.

"It's my duty as a philosophy major to exorcise you plebeians of all your ignorant ways," he says with a certain pleasure.

I'm never sure whether his arrogance is sarcasm or if his ego really is the size of Antarctica.

"If I put up a poster of the Loch Ness Monster, will it act like garlic and drive you and your vampiric ways out of my bedroom?"

"And just how am I vampiric?" Micah asks, ignoring my not-so-subtle hint that he's overstayed his welcome and sitting down on my bed.

"You suck the life out of everything around you."

"Just because I have a lower tolerance for ignorance than most people doesn't make me some kind of demon."

"Weeeeeell…"

Micah ignores this.

"If *this* was all there was to life," I gesture vaguely at the room we're sitting in, part of a grungy apartment that looks even cheaper than the $350 rent would suggest, "we're hosed."

"So maybe we're hosed."

"Or maybe you should keep your opinions to yourself."

"Defensiveness is a fairly immature way to admit that you're wrong."

Micah can be real annoying when he wants to be.

"So what makes you so sure there *isn't* anything else out there?" I prod in an effort to irritate him back.

Micah leans back against the wall, and it dawns on me with deep foreboding that this is exactly the question he was trying to bait out of me.

"People believe in the supernatural because it makes them feel better about their boring, meaningless lives. It's just a way for you people to lie to yourselves about the things you don't want to face."

"That's better than giving up!"

Micah stands up and heads for the door.

"If you're so desperate to believe in fantasies that your only way of getting through life is to cling to things that you already know perfectly well aren't real, it sounds like you already have."

I hate him sometimes.

After about a minute of wallowing in Micah's mic drop, I decide suddenly that being in different rooms is not nearly enough separation. I grab the garbage can and dash out the door before he can come up with something else he wants to talk about.

The sunset is in full bloom now, and I have to squint and turn my head sideways to keep its dying light from getting in my eyes. A tangy barbeque smell wafts toward me from somewhere over by apartment 9. Girls' voices chatter in the distance. One of them even sounds a little like *her* voice. No, not the one the title of this book is referring to. The other one.

"But I don't think he said anything, and then--" The girl trails off as she notices my arrival. "Hi, Levi!" It *is* her. My insides freeze over.

"Hey, Mara."

Her friend reads the room and scurries away.

"What are you up to?" I ask.

"Nothing much, just a study break. How about you?"

"Taking out the trash." I nod down at the overflowing receptacle in my arms.

It's the perfect opportunity. I have to ask her for her number. *Now.* I will my lips to form the required words, but they won't budge. I stall for time. "How did your Calc test go?"

"Pretty good. I messed up one or two questions, but I thought it was going to be a lot worse."

"That's good." My frozen insides start to crack under the strain. *Ask her now!* I scream at myself. *Now!*

"Anything else new?"

"No, not really." We stand there a few seconds more until the silence rots and turns awkward.

"Well, I'd better get inside," she says. "I have a lot of homework to get done."

I nod dumbly as she ducks inside the door. I am a total failure. I am an awful, wretched specimen of humanity who not only cannot win an argument to save his life but also cannot hit the romantic side of a barn door. My insides groan as suddenly being out here in the growing twilight seems as intolerable as having another chat with Micah.

Campus it is, then.

I never go to campus at night. Not because I can't, but because I'm not all that fond of being surrounded by so many people. This time, however, the encroaching darkness wipes all thought from my mind and replaces it with eerie melancholy. At moments like these, it's particularly easy to believe that Micah is right; life is just an unending hamster wheel of tedium that ultimately means nothing. To be honest, I tend to feel that way more than I'd like to admit.

I always walk to campus. That's not because I particularly like the exercise, but because I don't own a car. The reason is both financial and complicated. Regardless, it's hard not to bemoan it a little as it begins to drizzle lightly. If only I'd remembered to bring a jacket.

As I approach the library, it becomes obvious to me that it's going to be a chore to get anything done in my current state of mind. I head up to my favorite spot on the second floor, trying to clear my mind. The library isn't exactly packed, but it's clear that there are plenty of my fellow students who disagree with me about the ills of spending time on campus. I take a table by the European Language collection and start trying to remember the difference between a phylum and a genus.

For a while I'm able to keep myself on task through sheer willpower, but after about three hours, my attention begins to wane. I glance around the room and notice that only a handful of people are still here.

Scratching the back of my head, I exert a superhuman effort to bring my thoughts back into focus. I succeed marginally, but my attention is still scattered about like so much dry alfalfa on a windy day. Then I see her.

She's sitting on one of the far tables on the right, long blond hair tucked behind ears that are currently sporting a pair of ear buds. Her left hand sputters over the keyboard of a laptop that's kicked up onto one leg while the other arm dangles limply over the back of the chair. She's oozing so much "I don't care" energy that it makes me wonder why she's in the library in the first place. She's wearing a university hoodie and a Covid-style mask that covers all of her face but her eyes, which I realize with a start are *purple*. Purple! I wonder what kind of contacts she uses. She's staring right at me. Somehow it isn't awkward.

There's this crushing yet fragile sort of sadness to her, a cavernous, delicate agony that almost makes me want to run over and ask her what's wrong even though she's a complete stranger.

I give her a little wave, not really sure why she's looking over here. Just then an older man, likely part of the library staff, approaches her.

"Would you please turn that down?"

She looks up at him and freezes. That's a little odd as the request is quite reasonable; the music from her ear buds is so loud that I can hear it from where I'm sitting.

Then her skin goes pale and she starts shaking so violently I can see it from clear over here. Is she having a seizure? I leap to my feet and bridge the distance in a flash, scrambling for my phone in case I need to call 911. The library staff member backs up a step, looking terrified. The girl has her arms up over her head as if to ward off evil spirits. By now all the students in the vicinity are all turning to watch.

"Are you okay?" The staff member reaches toward her, and she jerks away like she's been stung. His knuckles whiten, eyes darting from her to the door to the surrounding audience. Flailing, he starts peppering her with questions.

"Do you need medication? Are you having an allergic reaction? Should we call an ambulance?"

At his last question, she shakes her head emphatically and leans back so far she topples out of her chair. Then she scrambles to her feet and backs up a few steps. She looks to be physically intact but is still staring at the poor staff member like he's a saber-tooth tiger.

"Is it a mental health crisis?" a bystander asks.

"Someone go get a counselor," says someone else. The staff member leaves to do just that, looking relieved to have someone to pass this off to. As soon as he's out of sight, the girl walks slowly back to the table and sits down again, although she is still shaking quite a bit. She's squeezing her hands into fists so hard that I'm worried that she's going to burst a blood vessel. All the attention on her is probably making it worse.

"Give her some space please," I find myself saying after a moment's hesitation. "Clear out, everyone." I shoo them away until it's just me, her, and the whole of the second floor European language study area.

"Thank you," she says to me finally.

"Sure."

I stand there awkwardly, wondering if I should go too. After fifteen minutes I'm about ready to do just that when two women in professional attire and badges with CAPS written on the front enter with the librarian. As soon as the girl sees him, she starts shaking again.

Seeing this, the older of the two women steps toward him and whispers something in his ear. He nods, and the two of them head back the way they came.

The younger woman, who is in her late 20's, turns and walks towards us.

"Nice to meet you," she says pulling up a chair. "I'm Amber, and we're from Counseling and Psychological Services here at the university. I understand that you've been having a rough night."

I feel a bit caught in the crossfire here, but Amber, probably assuming that I'm a friend or family member, points me toward a nearby chair. I take it, unsure of what I've just gotten myself into.

"What's been going on?" she asks.

The girl doesn't answer, although her shaking has decreased somewhat, and she's not hyperventilating anymore.

"You don't feel up to talking?"

More silence.

"You don't have to tell us everything, but we do need to collect a little information just to make sure you're in a safe place and have all the support that you need. Have you had any thoughts of wanting to go to sleep and not wake up again? You can nod or shake your head if that works better."

The girl nods.

"You have had thoughts like that?"

She nods again.

"Have you had any thoughts of suicide?"

The girl shakes her head no.

"Any thoughts like that in the past?"

Nod.

"How recently?"

"It's been a few years," she says quietly, speaking for the first time. Her voice has a certain raspy quality to it, as if she's been sick recently.

"Any suicide attempts or a step or two in that direction?"

Shake.

"All right. Thank you for answering my questions even though you don't feel much like talking to me today. Let's do a quick safety plan and see about getting you set up with a therapist, and I'll be on my way."

Amber has the girl fill out a list of warning signs and coping skills. She still says next to nothing but dutifully writes down a few things.

"Now put down some names of people you can call when you're having a hard time."

The girl stops and stares down at the paper. At this point the older of the two women, having presumably finished her conversation with the librarian, walks back and rejoins us.

"You can include people that you can confide in, like family, friends, or professors you trust," prompts Amber. "Or you can put down people you wouldn't necessarily share everything with but who you could call to distract yourself for a while if you needed it, like classmates or roommates."

The girl again stares blankly down at the paper.

"Neighbors, cousins, family friends from where you grew up?" Amber suggests, jaw tightening slightly. I'm dumbfounded. This girl has literally no one in the entire world she can call? Surely they won't cart her away somewhere if she can't come up with anyone, right?

"I was able to pull up her records," says the older woman. "If she can't come up with at least one name, we can reach out to her parents and see if they can check in with her regularly to make sure she's doing okay."

At this the girl's shoulders suddenly tense again.

"What about him?"

All eyes in the room are drawn the length of her index finger and then along the imaginary line extending from it into thin air several yards until it arrives at my chest.

"Who are you?" Amber asks me.

"I'm her friend," I say immediately without really knowing why. "My name's Levi," I add quickly as if I'm introducing myself to the crisis staff. In reality I'm saying my name out loud so the girl can write it down because if she has to ask for it, it will be a dead giveaway that she doesn't know me from Adam.

The lines that had slowly been forming on Amber's forehead slowly relax.

"Thank you, Levi, I really appreciate that," she says. "I'll need you to take especially good care of your friend here this semester, okay? Can you do that for me?"

I nod like I know exactly what I'm doing.

"It sounds like you're the only one she has in her life right now, so you're going to have a huge impact on how things go for her. And if anything else comes up, feel free to reach out to us at the counseling center."

They try to set the girl up with a therapist, but she tells them that she's not ready for that yet, and they seem to accept her answer. Then suddenly they're gone, and it's just the two of us sitting alone in the now-empty European Language section.

I should feel put upon, but I don't. There's something about that dull ache that I can still see in her eyes that feels familiar, somehow, even though I haven't had to deal with any mental health stuff myself.

"Well that was dumb," the girl says.

"I guess I should give you my number in case you need anything," I return.

"Buzz off."

"But she said—"

"I don't care what she said."

I should feel put out by that, but there's something about that look in her eyes that I can't quite put my finger on.

She sees me watching.

Our irises crash in an exploding kaleidoscope of sheer awareness. You know that mask you always wear in public? The one you use to keep everyone an arm's length away from your deepest insecurities? Well, for the briefest moment this girl in front of me, in contrast with the literal physical mask on her face, lets the emotional one slip. Suddenly I can see a *depth* to her heartache that hints at layer upon layer of further suffering stretching almost as far as the eye can see.

And then, down another layer still and almost out of sight, I see a light. A pure radiant beam of energy that sets my mind on fire. It's warm, bright, piercing. Everything I want my life to be but isn't. More precious than gold.

This isn't some kind of love-at-first-sight moment. What I'm feeling isn't hormones. But it is incredibly special. I want to cup her light gently in my hands, protect it from anything that could possibly try to hurt it.

As one, we break eye contact and turn away. The girl starts packing up, obviously intent on heading out soon.

For reasons I can't explain, the thought of her leaving and disappearing without a trace terrifies me. I scramble to get my stuff together so I can go with her, but she's already halfway out the door.

"Wait!"

I jog after her.

It's raining much more heavily now as I burst out the front door of the library. What with the buildings around me so completely devoid of life due to the late hour and the copious amount of precipitation, campus now feels otherworldly. After a few hurried glances, I spy the girl in the distance and walk quickly over to her.

"Hey—"

"Can't you take a hint?"

I stop.

"Buzz off," she says.

"Look, if you need anything--"

"I don't. Mind your own business."

My jaw clenches. Despite my fear of losing whatever magic spell this girl possesses, I know instinctively that this isn't something I can force. My heart sinks.

"Okay, fine. You don't want me in my life. I can respect that. Just promise me you'll reach out if you need something."

I scribble my digits on the first thing I can find and hand it to her. She doesn't take it.

"I'm not the kind of person you want to be around."

What a harsh thing to say about yourself.

"I'll be the judge of that, thank you very much," I say.

She looks away.

"Actually I do have a few people I talk to. I just didn't mention them because it was none of their business."

Silence reigns on.

"I can handle it."

More silence.

"Please just go."

I turn to leave.

"Look, thank you, all right?" she says, looking me in the eye for the first time. Her gaze is soft and hesitant, as if she's treading on unfamiliar ground. "If you see me again on campus, come and say hi. But I'm doing just fine. Really, I am. I know I can be a bit of a downer, but I'm not going to do anything stupid, I promise."

Something feels off about this, but she does actually look a lot better than before.

She tosses something into the trash can and starts off again. This time I let her go. I guess this is where this story ends, which is a pity because it would be nice to have a chance for her light to rub off on me. Also, I'd rather like to help her. There's nothing I can do about it, though.

Well, it's not like the trip home is getting any shorter or my shoulders any drier, so I hoist my backpack higher up my back and step towards the crosswalk that will lead me home. Suddenly a glint of something white catches my eye from the depths of the trash can. As I peer into it, my stomach does a backflip. I look around for the girl again, but she's nowhere to be seen. This isn't good. This isn't good at all. At the bottom of the receptacle, already sodden from the heavy rain, is a single slip of paper that changes everything.

It's her safety plan.

Chapter 2

The next morning I approach Micah during breakfast. As loathe as I am to admit it, he's the smartest person I know, and therefore the best chance of finding the girl from yesterday.

"If you wanted to find a specific student on campus, how would you do it?"

Micah eyes me over his bowl of unsweetened bran flakes.

"What for? You got your eye on someone?"

I almost lie and say yes to throw him off the scent, but the idea of him thinking he knows something about my love life is more than I can handle.

"There's someone I want to help."

Micah gives me a look that makes me want to die inside.

"Did they ask for help?"

"...No."

His scowl deepens.

"You're not getting some kind of White Knight Complex, are you?"

"What do you mean?"

"You know those people who go to Africa all high and mighty thinking they can change the world and then end up building a homeless shelter on top of the only water source? It's super condescending."

He says this with the air of someone picking at a particularly interesting scab.

"Uh..." I stammer, trying desperately to remain afloat in the conversation.

"So what do you know about this person? Name, major, any clubs they're a part of?"

"They, uh, have blonde hair?"

"There are a million people with blonde hair that go here."

I could tell him about the purple eyes, but for some reason I want him to know as little about her as possible.

"Yeah, I don't think it's doable," says Micah, taking another bite of bran flakes. "There's like 30K people who go here. If they're in a different major, they might not even go to the same parts of campus that you do. Maybe they're part time and take one class a week. Or maybe they're one of those students who is always working," his eyes flick to the third bedroom down the hall. "Or MIA." They flick to the fourth.

"You should give it up. There are plenty of straight women out there who are so desperate not to be lonely that they'd fall for anyone with a Y chromosome."

A little irked by the fact that Micah still thinks I'm in this for romance, I shove my bowl in the sink and head to class. No, that actually isn't what is irritating me. It's the fact that he called my wanting to help someone condescending.

*He has a way taking anything beautiful and **grinding** it to dust. He's one to talk about being condescending!*

Is what I'm trying do condescending? I'm doubting myself now. It's not like the girl was exactly clamoring for my help yesterday. But it's also true that there isn't anyone else who can step in right now but me.

So I do the only thing I can think of: Having reached campus early, I wander around, scanning the faces I pass for a tell-tale hint of blonde or violet. Maybe she eats breakfast at the food court? Nope. Maybe she jogs at the stadium track in the mornings? No luck there either.

I wander through a few of the humanities buildings on the off chance Micah is right and she is in a completely different major. The trickle of students on the walkways around me gradually thickens into a flood. I check the time on my phone and groan. It is time to go to class.

I don't hate class generally. It's this specific class that I'm dreading with the fury of a thousand suns. The one I'm heading to right now is the bane of a science major's existence and the killer of many a med school application: Organic Chemistry. The class has well over a hundred students in it and meets in a small auditorium in the building that houses most of the hard science courses. I sit about two-thirds of the way in the back, far enough to reduce my chances of being called on to answer a question but not so far back that I am in too much danger of falling asleep.

Up front, Dr. Sato is readying a stack of papers that looks particularly ominous. I pull out my notebook and prepare for the bloodbath. The girl next to me with long, light brown hair gives me a knowing smile.

"Maybe we'll get lucky and have only a three-hour-long assignment today."

I nod back.

"The length of it isn't what I'm worried about."

Dr. Sato stands up and approaches the podium. A hush reminiscent of a funeral home washes over the room.

"This class," she begins, slowly pacing the front of the class with the air of a general sending her troops to war, "does not have a final exam."

Now the silence morphs to bewilderment. It's too good to be true, right? No one dares cheer for fear their cautious optimism will immediately be dashed. I had been wondering why she had left the bit of the syllabus labeled "Final" so mysteriously vague when she ran us through it last week. Now it seems we are about to find out.

"No final? Yeah right," says the kid in front of me.

Dr. Sato pauses like a game show host ready to reveal who's getting kicked off the island. That tells me all I need to know. We're doomed.

"This class has a final presentation." Around the room there are nods of grudging acceptance. That was to be expected. But Dr. Sato is not done.

"A *group* presentation that will be worth forty percent of your grade." There is an audible groan. She has done it again. Despite all odds, she has taken our expectations of how awful this was going to be and driven over them with a dump truck.

"You will sort yourselves into groups of three. I will pick the topics. You will write a well-researched five-page paper and deliver an exemplary twenty-minute presentation. In order to ensure that everyone in your group participates, you must all participate equally in the presentation. If one of you doesn't pull their weight, let me know," she waves a menacing finger towards us, "and I'll fail them."

"She's just sore because everyone ditches the lectures," says the kid in front of me. I notice that he is much quieter with his comments this time. I glance around the room with growing dread. I don't know anyone here. How am I supposed to pick who to stake my medical career on?

"Do you want to join a group with me?" the brown-haired girl from earlier asks me.

"Sure."

"Great. Who else should we get?"

The kid in front of us takes his cue and turns around.

"I'll jump in too. I'm Raymond." He is built like a linebacker with a bit of a drawl to his voice, though it is faint enough that I can't place it.

"Levi."

"And I'm Lindsay," says the girl. "We should exchange contact info. We can meet at my apartment to write the paper, if you want. Are you all chem majors?" I shake my head.

"Exercise science."

Raymond whistles. "Premed?"

"Yup."

"Condolences."

"The sympathy is appreciated," I sigh.

"We'd all better do a good job, then. Your future's on the line here."

"No pressure," Lindsay laughs. I decide that I've gotten lucky with my group. Then a thought strikes me.

"Hey, have either of you seen a girl around campus with purple eyes?" Raymond squints like he hasn't heard me right.

"Purple eyes? Is that a thing?"

"I don't know. Contacts, I assume?"

"No, actually I've heard of that before," says Lindsay. "Wasn't there an actress who had that?"

"Uh--"

"Yeah, yeah," says Raymond. "Didn't she have some kind of genetic mutation?"

"Ah—well, anyway, have you seen anyone like that?"

"Naw, but that doesn't mean anything," says Raymond. "I could hit the broad side of a barn and not realize it."

"I haven't either," says Lindsay. "Sorry."

At this point I'm not really sure whether it's worth it to keep looking for Mystery Girl. I want to ask her about throwing away her safety plan to make sure that it isn't a sign of something more serious. On the other hand, how is it possible for a person who has obviously experienced more suffering than I ever will to also have so much light about her? Does that mean she is actually okay after all, and her mental turmoil isn't actually as bad as I thought? Also, it's not like I can put my whole life on hold for someone I don't even really know. Probably the most reasonable course of action at this point is to keep an eye out for her and hope that I get lucky.

It's raining again as I leave campus, even harder than yesterday. It matches my state of mind perfectly. Still, my homework isn't going to do itself. So instead of trying to find the needle in the proverbial haystack for a few more hours, I abandon my hopeless quest and march through the torrential downpour toward home. I remembered my jacket today, but it almost doesn't matter because of how hard it's coming down. At least it's warm rain.

I cross the street at my usual crosswalk and begin my trek across town, glancing furtively at the cars driving by. I hope none of them stop and offer me a ride. Those situations always end up so awkward.

After a few minutes of walking, I spy a car on the shoulder of the road with its hazard lights on. At first I don't think anything of it besides a bit of sympathetic commiseration with my fellow victim of mother nature. Then I see figure huddled up against the front wheel closest to the sidewalk, and suddenly it's as if the needle has leapt from the haystack and jabbed me in the finger. It's the girl from the library, wrestling with a car jack like it's some kind of vicious serpent.

"Need help?"

She looks up at me over the edge of her mask and glares at me. Then she stands up and starts rummaging around in the back seat of the car. Glancing through the window, I can see that she is trying to cram a large quantity of sheet music into an enormous instrument case. As big as the case is, there are way more papers than will fit in it, so she unzips her backpack and starts stuffing them in there too. It's clearly a lost cause, as her backpack is already full to capacity. I'm not completely sure what she intends to do with them in a car that isn't going anywhere anytime soon.

"I have extra room in my backpack if you need it."

She glances up at me.

"Buzz off."

She keeps stuffing her backpack like a Thanksgiving turkey. I look on, curious what her plan is. The girl forces a few more pages into the instrument case and slams it shut with effort. Then she hooks one arm around a backpack strap and the other through the handle of the instrument case and starts staggering down the sidewalk, pausing just long enough to close the car door with a foot. Is she serious right now?

She makes it only a few yards before the inevitable happens. The instrument case thumps into a power pole and bursts open, spraying the air with papers. I leap forward and grab as many as I can, shoving a sheaf of them back into the instrument case. A number of them make contact with the wet sidewalk and I hurry and scoop them up, cramming the rest into the back seat of her car. I look around hurriedly to see if I missed any.

Then I notice that the girl isn't helping me. She's collapsed into a little puddle of goo on the sidewalk, backpack still dangling uselessly from her forearm. It suddenly occurs to me that the fact that she was trying to change a flat tire by herself in the rain means that her line yesterday about having people that she talks to regularly was probably a lie.

I sit down next to her. The concrete sidewalk is so wet, it soaks my jeans in seconds, but it's not as if I don't have several other pairs waiting for me at home. The girl looks up, surprised.

"What's up?" I ask.

She narrows her eyes but doesn't shrink away from me. She also doesn't say anything, but for some reason I don't think it's out of annoyance.

"Perfect day for a rainstorm, am I right?"

Again she says nothing. I lean back against a power pole and wait.

"You sure know how to organize a girl's sheet music," she says finally, glancing at the piles of paper strewn every which way around the back of the car.

I wink.

"It's a trade secret."

"This is the point where you're supposed to pull out the umbrella and the cheesy pickup line, right?"

"Must have forgotten that part."

"Well maybe you should start remembering it."

She realizes what she's just implied right after the words leave her mouth and quickly backtracks.

"On second thought, if you ever do that, I'll rip you a new one."

"Understood."

We sit there for a while longer, getting wetter and wetter.

"You can have a ride if you promise not to leave cooties all over my seat."

Cooties? What on earth?

"Cross my heart."

I look over at her front tire, which is flatter than a bad string on an underwater ukulele.

"Reckon we can find a video online about how to take care of that?"

A half an hour, many gallons of rainwater, and a few stubborn lug nuts later, we heave ourselves into the car, wondering why we bothered to shower this morning.

"What's your name?" I ask once we're settled.

"If I tell you that, I might have to talk to you again."

"Ouch. And here I thought I was growing on you."

"You are. Like an algae."

Her violet eyes are smiling slightly over the top of her Covid mask. Maybe now's a good time to ask.

"Why did you throw away your safety plan?"

She takes a moment to respond.

"Why do you think? Because it's dumb."

She says it lightheartedly enough that my fear for her more or less dissipates. Still, it's hard to believe that something like that wasn't significant on *some* level.

I abruptly realize that we've driven into the seedier end of town. Not too far from campus, but not exactly a hotbed of collegiate activity either. On the left is a string of particularly unsavory bars next to a mortuary that looks like it's got one foot in the grave itself. Across the street on the right is the most decrepit little apartment complex I've ever seen. One of the windows on the second floor is boarded up, and the fire escape along the far side is more rust than steel. *Who in their right mind would live in a place like that?* I wonder.

Then Mystery Girl turns into the parking lot, and my question is immediately answered. Then she freezes, seeming to realize only now where she's driven by force of habit. She groans and thumps the steering wheel with her forehead.

"I don't suppose I can convince you that this is my cousin's place."

"Nope," I rejoin. "Don't worry, though. My lips are sealed."

"They'd better be."

She relaxes slightly, but not much. It's obvious that she's still kicking herself.

"I suppose I could let you in," she says reluctantly.

An hour ago I would have said yes without thinking. But there's a certain trodden-on look in her eye that makes me want to give her a break, to let her save face.

"Only if you want to."

"I don't"

"Then don't."

"I can't just bring you all the way here just to take you back again," she says, clearly shocked to hear the words come out of her mouth.

"Sure you can. You don't owe me anything."

"Weren't you the one falling over yourself trying to be my friend yesterday?"

"Funny, I remember, *you* being the one trying to convince people I was your best buddy. And yes, I do want to be your friend. But isn't a part of that knowing when to give you space?"

She pauses, deep in thought.

"It's funny. I've gotten so used to people shoving their heads into my business anytime they hear the words 'mental health' that now that I find someone who's not biting my head off about it, I'm not sure what to say."

"Then don't say anything. Just tell me where you want to meet up to hang tomorrow."

"That would be saying something, you doofus."

"You know what I mean."

"Meet me by the practice rooms in the music building at seven," she says finally.

"Sounds good," I say, "See you there."

Chapter 3

The next evening Mystery Girl doesn't show. I'm not necessarily expecting to be stood up, but as the minutes tick by without any sign of her, I find that I'm not surprised either. I am disappointed, though. I was kind of hoping that she'd open up enough for me help her out a bit. As I think about it now, stepping out into growing twilight, I'm not sure who I was kidding. *Of course* she isn't going to let some random stranger prance right into her life. People just aren't like that in real life.

Today the coming dusk feels much less mystical than it did on Monday. Is that because the magic is out of my line of sight at the moment? Or because it was only an illusion to begin with? Somehow I know that Micah would approve of this line of thinking, which doesn't improve my mood at all.

As I near the one of the main crosswalks out of campus, a somber resignation settles over me. Everything feels so *useless.*

My foot hits the curb at an odd angle, and I know I'm in trouble. My self-pity partying is violently interrupted as my shoulder has an inglorious meeting with the asphalt. My lab book, which I had been holding in my arms, goes flying. My knee touches down next, hitting the pavement so hard I audibly gasp. My only consolation is that campus is so desolate this time of day that there isn't any traffic, and therefore there's no one around to witness my ignominious demise.

I lie there for a second, just wallowing in my misery. I don't particularly want to get up again. I suppose I'd better start thinking about it, though.

"Are you okay?"

I leap back to my feet, blushing furiously. Where did my lab book get to? I look around frantically for it, anxious to get out of here already.

"Here."

I look up to see my spiral bound notebook being proffered toward me with a hand attached to it. It's a woman with blonde hair. Of course it is. The universe is mocking me now. I take my lab book back with a little more force than intended and finally turn to meet her gaze. Her *violet* gaze. She must have been waiting at a distance, trying to decide whether or not to show.

"You stood me up," I say.

"So?" Her voice is much colder than yesterday.

"So I'm disappointed."

"Well boo hoo."

I'm confused.

"Did I do something wrong?"

"No," she snaps. Then, slightly less heatedly, "You're bleeding, by the way."

I look down to see a giant scarlet tear where my jeans and the ground have gone to fisticuffs.

"Ah."

"There's a nurse's station right over there. They probably have band-aids."

The girl grabs my hand like it's something she does every day and pulls me over to the building she indicated. Inside she leaves me on a bench and disappears for a moment before returning with the goods. I patch up my knee, mind spinning like a revolving door full of overly energetic squirrels. First she goes and gets all snippy with me, and now she's rushing about bringing me bandages. What's going on with her?

"Did you wait long for me?" she asks stiffly.

"A few minutes. It's okay. I needed a break after such a long day."

I'm downplaying it a bit, though I'm not sure why.

"And then I come crashing into you like a lunatic and make it ten times worse."

"Wait!" Suddenly I remember a slight bump from behind right before I'd stepped on the curb. "That wasn't your fault. I just slipped."

"Right." Her eyes are dark pits of self-loathing.

"No, really! I stepped off the curb weird."

"Sure. I get it."

This isn't working. In an effort to derail her inner hate train, I quickly change the subject.

"What kind of contacts do you use?"

"I don't use contacts."

"Wait, why are your eyes that color then?"

"It's a genetic mutation," she answers stiffly.

"They're amazing."

"Thanks," she says soullessly.

"No, really!" I say a second time, desperate now. "I've never seen anything like them."

She just stares at me.

"You can't take a compliment, can you?"

She gives me a look of old, crusted pain that somehow serves as more of an answer than a verbal response would have been. Where was that light in her eyes from before? I don't see even a hint of it now.

"You let me blow you off like it didn't matter!" she seethes.

Why is that something to get upset about?

"I thought you said you liked me giving you space."

"Yes. No! You just suck, that's all! No, it's me. I suck."

"I don't think you suck."

"I don't care what you think."

"Will you tell me your name now?"

"No. Buzz off."

Mystery Girl gets up to leave. She makes it as far as the door and then stops, leaning against the door frame with her back to me.

"Sorry for yelling at you. I'm just...so *tired*," Sigh. "See you around, Levi."

A solitary teardrop graces the carpet at her feet, and she's gone with the swishing of the shutting door behind her.

She remembers my name. I find that odd, somehow. I stare after her. I don't blame her for getting angry; I can see how confused she is by life right now. I'm just not sure that I'm the one that can change that, as much as I'd like to be. I'm completely and totally out of my depth.

I approach the door and lean against the frame at the same spot she did but for a completely different reason. She just seemed so...beaten down. Resigned. Like life has kicked her in the teeth so many times that she's gotten used to living in the fetal position. Like she's spent a lifetime banging her head against the wall only to fall further and further and further behind.

Is that what happens to those of us who dare to hope for some type of meaning in this world?

I catch myself tangled up in the thought and quickly shake free from it. That's a question to consider when I'm in a better frame of mind. I stick my lab book underneath my arm and step out into the night.

Chapter 4

When I get home, the apartment is desolate. Somehow Micah still mocks me even in his absence because for some reason, the solitude bothers me tonight. At first it had seemed obvious to me that this was the right way to play it: Be consistent enough to convince Mystery Girl to rely on me, but aloof enough that she won't feel pushed into it. Now, though, I'm not sure. What is so awful about insisting that she give herself more credit? I kind of understand, but I kind of don't. It's a good thing I don't have any homework due tomorrow because I don't think I'd be able to focus on it even if I did.

A door opens down the hall, and I nearly leap out of my skin. It's not Micah. It's Mason, one of the roommates I never see. He graduated from the same school that we go to a year prior and got a job as a mental health therapist at a local clinic. Since we live off campus, he hasn't had to move out yet. I mostly think of him as living proof that the unending slog that is school actually ends at some point. Other than that, I don't really know him.

"Joining us in the land of the living, huh?" I comment.

He chuckles, sitting down at the table.

"Yeah, I thought I might. What's your name again? Liam?"

"Levi."

"Ah, that's right." Mason isn't exactly stocky but he has a certain presence to him that makes him seem big.

He has dark hair that flows down past his ears and piercing eyes that make me want to put on something X-ray-proof.

"So how's it hanging?"

"Ah—good." I stare off into space, not sure what else to say to him. Wait a minute.

"How do you help someone?" I query tentatively.

"What kind of help?"

"That's the problem. I don't know."

"Well that makes it harder."

I try again.

"Have you ever known someone that you wanted to help *really* badly?"

Mason gives me a look.

"Yes," he says slowly. "A long time ago."

I cock my head.

"Don't you do it for a living?"

A thin smile flitters across his face.

"Yes, but it's a bit different than what I think you're talking about. It's gotten personal."

I feel a bit weird about that.

"I mean, I do feel bad for her, but I wouldn't call it *personal*."

Mason traces the grain of the table with a finger.

"You just told me she's important to you. How is that not personal?"

I've only implied that it's a girl we're talking about, but Mason's picked up on it immediately.

"I'm not going to lose my head over it."

"I'm not saying you are. I'm just saying that you've gotten invested in how this turns out."

"I guess..."

"That's not a bad thing. If anything, I wish there were more people who cared."

I stand up and start to pace, the nervous energy getting the better of me.

"So what do I do about it?"

"Well, it's hard to say without knowing the specifics."

"She seems so *angry* sometimes," I realize suddenly. "Not at me, just at, I don't know, herself, I guess."

"That's something. Whenever you see anger, that means that there's some kind of pain there. And anytime there's pain, there's also something that is loved. If you can help her tap into that, it might do something for her."

Mason has just somehow taken the conversation from barely knowing my name to probing the depths of my soul in five minutes flat. I guess that's just what therapists do. He slides back in his chair.

"Look, one of the things I've learned from having deep conversations with people every day is that dreams tend to fade as we grow older. As children we're so alive with vitality and hope for the future, but the irony is that when we get old enough to actually start to *achieve* some of the things we've always dreamed about, our lives often become so driven by what we should do or what we think we should want that we lose our grip on what was most important to us. But in *your* eyes," he points at me, "I see some of the fire hasn't yet gone out. Whatever this person means to you, it's a rare and beautiful thing. Be careful, yes, but don't you *dare* throw it away."

With that he retreats back into his room, leaving me once more at the mercy of my thoughts. Unfortunately for me, that has become an increasingly dangerous place for me to be. In some ways I feel more confused than ever. Strangely, though, a part of me now feels at peace. I wonder briefly how Mason would weather a Micah special. I'd rather like to see that.

* * *

For the next week, I keep an eye out for Mystery Girl whenever I'm on campus. At first I'm strangely optimistic about running into her again. I'm not exactly combing the school for her, but I do spend a little more of my time on campus and keep my eyes peeled.

But as the week drags on without a hint of violet irises, it starts to feel like I'm once again at a dead end. I find myself doing a lot of my homework on the second floor of the library in hopes that she'll return. I always leave campus by the same crosswalk where I ran into her. It occurs to me that maybe she's avoiding those places on purpose.

On Friday I meet up with Raymond and Lindsay to start our group project. We're just meeting in the science building, so the odds of the girl showing up here are pretty low. I practically live in that place, and it would be fairly obvious if she did too. As soon as I enter the room, my shoulders subtly tense, as they do every time my academic life is backed up against a wall. Raymond and Lindsay seem slightly nervous as well, although not as much as I am.

I pull out the rubric and read through it in painstaking detail. There's an awful lot to this project.

"Right. We got assigned elimination reactions. We have to talk about the difference between E1 and E2 reactions and then pick one of each to show examples. Then we have to explain the types of factors that slow them down and speed them up."

"For E2 we could talk about 2-Bromopropane reacting with ethoxide," Raymond suggests.

"Yeah, but there will be a lot of SN2 reactions to worry about with that one. Maybe we should pick one that's simpler."

"What about tert-butoxide?" suggests Lindsay. "It's a lot bigger, so it's more difficult for the oxygen to act as a nucleophile."

I nod.

"Yes, but we should also talk about how much heat is involved because elimination reactions increase entropy so much. Do you want to find some research papers on that reaction?"

"Sure."

"Then Raymond, if you wouldn't mind looking at a couple other reactions for E1?"

"That's fine."

"Once you've done that, send the sources over to me and I'll write it--"

"Wait," Lindsay cuts in, "You're going to write the whole thing yourself?"

"I mean, the research part really is a lot of work--"

"I'll write a section on E1 reactions. I don't mind," says Raymond.

"I mean, I guess I could--"

"I'll talk about the 2-Bromopropane and ethoxide reaction," says Lindsay. "Why don't you just cover E2 reactions generally and talk about the entropy changes like you were saying?"

I squirm a little inside.

"I don't mind writing it, really."

"Give it up," says Raymond. "We're not going to let you do it all yourself."

"Okay, well I guess I'll at least put it all together at the end so I can give it a thorough edit."

"Wait a second," says Lindsay. "Do you not trust us?"

"No, I do!" I say a bit too quickly.

"We got this, Bro," adds Raymond. "We're going to kill it. Don't sweat it." I purse my lips and nod begrudgingly. I hate giving up control of my grade to anyone else, especially to people I don't know well.

"By the way, did you ever find that person you were looking for with the purple eyes?" asks Lindsay.

"Yes, but I still don't know her name."

"Or her number, apparently."

"It's not like that! I just--" I suddenly realize that I can't fully explain the situation without giving up very personal information that isn't mine to share. "It was late, and I'd just happened to scrape my knee as I was leaving campus, so she got me a band-aid from the nurse's station."

Lindsay raises her eyebrow and Raymond adds:

"She couldn't have."

"Wait, why?"

"Because the nurse's station closes after hours."

That gives me pause. He's right. But if that's the case, how was she able to get in? Maybe she was lying about where she got the band-aid. But then—what, she carries one around in her back pocket?

"Maybe she found someone to unlock it for her?"

"Unlikely," says Raymond. "Anyone with access would have been long gone by then. My roommate works there, and he says everyone's out of there by four because there aren't many late afternoon classes."

"Wait," I say again slowly. "What type of students *can* access the nurse's station at night?"

"That's easy," says Lindsay.

"The ones in the nursing program."

Chapter 5

She's in the nursing program. That's potentially game-changing information, but do I dare use it? It's one thing to keep my eyes peeled for Mystery Girl as I go about my day, but pursuing this lead would mean that I'd be more actively seeking her out. Is that okay? I glance down at the rubric, but I'm now too distracted to focus.

"Ah, well, at this point I think we're pretty clear on what we're each doing for the assignment," I manage.

Lindsay gives me a knowing look that makes me want to shrivel up into a pile of goo.

I'm not in love with her, I promise!

"Let's meet again next week once we have our sources so we can get on the same page for the writing," she says.

After some thought, I head toward the building that houses the nursing department. This building in particular is one of the tallest on campus, ten stories tall but narrow, with each level small enough that only a handful of offices fit on each floor.

The directory indicates that floors 6-8 belong to nursing. I pick floor 7 because it's just a study area and I'm less likely to barge into a class of people giving injections or something. There are a few people wandering around up here, but not many, which is perfect. I choose someone at random who doesn't look too busy. I opt for a male because I figure they're less likely to give me weird looks in a much more female-dominated part of town.

"Hey, are you in the nursing program?"

The red-haired kid looks up at me and immediately proves me wrong by giving me a scathing glance. He nods silently.

"Do you know a girl with blonde hair and purple eyes?"

The kid looks at me like I have three heads and doesn't even bother to answer. I move on again, this time approaching a female student who looks more easy going.

"Hey, do you know anyone in your program with purple eyes?"

"Purple eyes? Like from contacts?"

"So that's a no then?"

I'm a little puzzled by this as I assume that's a distinctive enough feature for most people in her major to know her at least by sight. I'm thinking up a way to rephrase the question when I feel someone grab me by the shoulder.

"Fancy running into you here."

I whirl around and come face-to-face with...Mara.

"Wait, you're a nursing major? How did I not know that?"

"I'm just full of surprises, I guess. What brings you to the nursing department?"

I pause. Anyone else can think I'm crushing on Mystery Girl and it's fine, but I'm not about to let Mara get within a hundred miles of that idea.

"I was just looking for someone, but it looks like they aren't here," I answer as vaguely as I can, very aware that the girl I was just talking to is still listening. Mara eyes me suspiciously, but then inspiration strikes and I quickly add:

"It's fine, though. I'd rather run into you anyway."
Mara smiles.

"Well maybe we should do this on purpose sometime."

"Yeah." My brain falls out of my head as it realizes she's subtly encouraging me to ask her out and doesn't know what to do next. "Yeah we should," it manages.

The nursing student is still looking on, and I wish she'd take a hike. What kinds of dates do people go on anyway?

"Um, I'll uh, have to look at my schedule and get back to you."

Mara's eyes darken a little, and my heart sinks.

"All right," she says quietly.

I wrack my brain desperately to find something to save the situation, but she is already heading for the elevator.

"See you around," she says.

As soon as she is out of sight, I make a break for the stairs. If I take the elevator, I might run into her again, but I still need to leave as soon as possible. Finding the violet-eyed girl will have to wait for another day.

I no longer have the luxury of letting my nerves get in the way of trying my luck with Mara. If I don't ask her out ASAP, she's going to interpret what I just said as a rejection. But my dating experience is...let's just say sparser than Micah's credit hours in warmth and fuzziness. And speaking of Micah, he is literally the only person I can think of to ask for help. That's a lonely thought if I've ever had one. Maybe once I've proven to my father that I have what it takes to be a doctor, I'll be able to balance out my focus on school with a healthy dose of social life and maybe even find a friend or two.

I take my time walking home today, even though I'm in a hurry. That's how much I'm dreading this conversation with Micah. I can already imagine how much gloating he's going to be able to squeeze from each word.

Abruptly, I realize that the girl walking in front of me has long blonde hair and a backpack that looks awfully familiar. Wait, no way! Has lightning struck *again*? I hurry to catch up.

"Hey!"

The girl turns, and my eyes immediately leap up to meet hers. They're brown. I scramble to backpedal.

"Sorry, I thought you were someone I know."

"That's the lamest pickup line I've ever heard."

"It wasn't intended as one," I say. And then, as my way of screaming at the world, "Unless you want it to be."

She gives me a once-over.

"You'll do."

"I'll *do*? Talk about lame pickup lines."

She socks me in the shoulder, but not too hard.

"I actually did think you were someone I know," I say.

She socks me again, harder this time.

"Hey what's your name?"

"I'm Charlotte."

"Levi." It hits me that this might be the answer to my problems.

"You look like you go on a lot of dates."

"In a good way or a bad way?"

I wink ambiguously.

"So let's say I have someone I want to ask out. How do I not butcher it?"

"Well first of all, drop the dumb pickup lines."

"They seemed to work on you."

She sticks out her tongue at me.

"Seriously, though. And make sure you ask her on a date where you can actually talk to each other. No movie dates!"

"Noted."

"Anything else will probably be *passable,* but if you really want to kick things up a notch, you should pick something that she's already interested in."

"What if I don't know what she's interested in?"

Charlotte rolls her eyes like I'm the biggest imbecile on the planet.

"How have you gotten this far in life?"

"So you admit my progress is impressive."

"Yeah that smart aleck thing you have going on isn't going to get you very far. You have to be *smooth.*"

"Like you?"

"Yes. Anyway, if you don't know anything about her, it's better to go with something generic like grabbing dinner. You could ask her to some kind of event on campus, but that's a risk if you don't know what she's into."

Suddenly it hits me that this is a golden opportunity to have a contact on my phone other than the floating cloud of doom waiting for me at home.

"Cool, thanks. Hey, give me your digits. We should hang out sometime." I proffer my phone.

"Actually, you aren't so bad at this." She takes it and puts in her information. "By the way, the girl you're asking out isn't the one you thought I looked like, is it?"

"Ah, no. That was just someone I ran into the other day. By the way, you don't happen to know anyone with purple eyes, do you?"

Charlotte gives me a look I can't interpret.

"You're so smart and so dumb at the same time."

"No, I'm serious! She actually has purple eyes."

"Sounds like a real freak."

There's an edge to her voice that stops me in my tracks. I'm offended.

"You shouldn't be so quick to judge her. There's a lot more to her than meets the eye."

"Yeah, sure."

Charlotte leaves me stewing. She obviously knows Violet-Eyed Girl somehow. There's no way she would have gotten that worked up about people with purple eyes without having some kind of nasty history. Well, Mystery Girl can be a bit frosty sometimes, so maybe that isn't too surprising. As my finger hovers over the button to delete Charlotte's number, something hits me. Maybe she can tell me something about why Mystery Girl is hurting so much. Charlotte still seems to have a relatively high opinion of me, so it isn't impossible. So I shove down my unrealistically frigid anger and keep the number. I have a feeling she might be a tough nut to crack, but it might just be worth it.

When I get back, Micah's already there. I'm not going to be here for long because Charlotte just answered the questions I was going to ask him anyway and because stage two of Operation Ask Out Mara starts soon.

"Does true altruism actually exist?" he asks the second he sees me.

"Good afternoon to you too, Micah."

He catches me by the shoulder.

"Humans are inherently selfish creatures. They evolved to cooperate because it turned out to be the most effective way of looking out for number one."

I really don't want to deal with this right now, but probably the quickest way to get this over with will be to play along.

"That's dumb. There are plenty of people who donate to charities and run fundraisers and help little old ladies cross the street. You really think they're all doing that to get a tax break?"

Micah settles into his groove.

"People try to be nice because they want to pat themselves on the back or because they don't want to feel guilty. They don't *actually* care about anyone else.

They just think that helping someone is the quickest way to feel good."

"A lot of people care about their significant others."

Micah's grimace-like smile broadens.

"That's even worse. When was the last time you dated someone to figure out if *you* were the best person for *them*? Isn't it the opposite? And where does all the 'love' go when you get broken up with or cheated on? What if being in a relationship with them interferes with your career? Aren't you just going to dump them and find somebody else?"

I feel my temperature rise in spite of myself. Why did he have to get so intense about these things?

"Parents love their children!"

"Parents are evolutionarily programmed to feel guilty if they don't take care of their children. They see them as a way to live the life they never had and prove to the world that they're good enough. Using someone smaller and more vulnerable than you to make yourself feel less awful isn't 'good.'"

I sigh and throw in the towel.

"Are we done here?"

"Praising selflessness itself comes from selfishness. Like Neitzsche says," Micah whips open the appropriate textbook, "'The neighbor praises selflessness because it brings him advantages.'"

"Swell." I grab my athletics pass and a granola bar. "Send Neitzche my regards."

For once Micah actually seems a little bit put out as I make my exit, but my blood pressure is still high enough for me to know that his barbs, as always, have hit their mark.

* * *

The athletic center is bustling by the time I get there. We have a killer women's volleyball team. You can tell that just by the number of students they can pull out of their dorms on a weeknight. Thanks to Micah, my earlier enthusiasm for asking Mara out and the possibility of finding a way to help Violet-Eyed Girl has molted into wet ash. Still, my head is on a swivel as I make my way toward the student section. Mara is a big volleyball fan, and tonight's game is against a top-ten school. There's no way she won't be here. Wait a minute, I guess I know something that she's interested in after all. How about that?

I cross the whole student section without spotting her, so I head up to the far corner with the hope of picking her out as soon as she walks in.

The arena is a churning mass of humanity. It's so loud that I almost can't hear myself think. Despite my purpose here being anything but volleyball, I can't help but channel a bit of the electricity myself. Just like that, the malaise hanging over me from my dose of too much Micah slowly begins to melt away.

The volleyball team walks out onto the court, and the din swells to a roar. I keep my eyes on the aisles as there are still a number of people making their way to their seats. In the seating block farthest away from me a twosome, obviously a couple, makes their way to their seats. One section over, a blonde-haired girl is climbing the stairs. My heart leaps for a second before I realize that the person I'm looking at is much shorter than Purple-Eyed Girl. Fate's been picking on me a lot lately. I turn my head to look at the next aisle, and suddenly my heart pile drives into my stomach. It's her.

Mara.

I slowly rise to my feet, grateful that she's still far enough away not to see my legs shaking. I start toward her. Part of me hopes that space will magically stretch, and it will take me an eternity to get there, but unfortunately the laws of physics still seem to be working today. She's sitting towards the end of her row, but there's just enough space that I can probably squeeze onto the end of the row next to her. I'm on her aisle now.

"Ladies and Gentlemen, please rise for the National Anthem."

I freeze and whirl around, hand over my heart, thanking and cursing the universe in the same breath. The person singing is, of course, a female with blonde hair. Her voice is melodic and vibrant, but I don't have the presence of mind to appreciate it because my nerves mixed with the waiting are driving me bonkers. I squint my eyes against the glare of the spotlight.

"and the hooooome of the braaaaaaaaaaave!"

Finally it's over. Couldn't it have had just one more verse? The audience sits, and I resume my trek. I'm five rows above her. Now three. Just as I'm about to get within earshot, a guy that's about six feet tall leaps up three steps in a single bound and sits down next to her. Operation Ask Out Mara has just been spiked in the face. Now it's possible that the guy next to her isn't a date, but that isn't a risk I'm willing to take. Panicking, I slide into the first open seat I can find. My best bet is to wait it out and hope she either leaves by herself or gets up to go to the bathroom at some point. I guess I could swing by her apartment later...but the memory of my last encounter with her there was not exactly a pleasant one.

Amid my inner council of war, it's a minor miracle that I notice my phone vibrate. For a crazy split second I think that it might be Mara texting me. Then I remember that she doesn't even have my number yet. I slip my phone from my pocket.

It's *Charlotte*. What?

Meet me by the concession stand

No, seriously. What on earth is going on here? My eyes leap to the back of Mara's head. I'm not going to be able to do anything with this for the moment; I suppose I may as well see what Charlotte wants. I'll admit that I'm incredibly curious about the timing of this, and it's not like I'm actually going to be paying any attention to the game at this point anyway.

Still, it feels like I'm admitting defeat as I get up to leave. I promise myself that this isn't the end of Operation Ask Out Mara. The crowd groans as I reach the bottom of the stairs. The home team just lost a critical point. A smile slips across my face in spite of myself because it matches my mood so perfectly.

As I pass through the giant double doors leading out of the arena, the cacophony of the crowd instantly grows muted. There are a few odd people wandering about here and there, but the contrast with the crowded bleachers is —nice, honestly. I let out a breath that I hadn't realized I'd been holding. Somehow the prospect of talking to Charlotte feels substantially less daunting than interacting with Mara has ever been.

Ahead of me is the concession stand. Charlotte isn't there yet. I skirt around an advertisement for an art exhibition and head toward it, eyes peeled for her.

A swath of blond hair whooshes by me, and I turn to look instinctively. *Are you kidding me?* I yell internally at the universe. *Are you* SERIOUSLY *going to send me every single blonde-haired girl in the entire world except the one I'm--*

And then I see her eyes.

Chapter 6

I'm so blindsided that I almost miss my window before it's slammed shut again.

"Hey!" It comes out a little louder than I meant it to but still has the intended effect. Miracle Girl stops and turns around. She's wearing her mask, as always. I wonder what it's for.

"What are you doing here?" I cringe slightly at my choice of words, but I don't have time to come up with anything better. My brain is busy scrambling the conversation content unit but is still waiting for a response, so my mouth has just spit out the first thing that came to mind.

"Oh, you know, about ready to set up my own lemonade stand out here."

I'm not sure how to take that.

"Do you know Charlotte?"

Her eyes narrow.

"I hate her," she says with a vehemence that takes me aback.

"I mean, she's a bit judgmental, but I didn't think she was *that* bad. I bet you can get through to her."

To my absolute shock, Miracle Girl bursts out laughing.

"That would be a real miracle."

I...don't think I understand anything anymore.

"Are you a nursing student?"

"Why, do I look like one?"

"Wait, you're not? How did you get into the nursing station after hours, then?"

She puts a finger to her masked face and winks.

"It's a secret."

So, uh, what's the plan here? My eyes dart to the poster behind her, and I suddenly hear myself saying:

"Do you want to go on a date to the art exhibition?"

This time I've managed to shock both of us at the same time. She looks away. For the first time she seems unsure of herself.

"Okay."

My mind, still reeling from the consequences of its own antics, takes a second to parse the implications of her response. She looks at the poster.

"Thursday at seven, right? I'll meet you by the mammoth statue in front of the art building."

She whirls around and heads back the way she came as I try to figure out whether I've made a terrible mistake.

Operation Ask Out Mara is officially on hold. There's no way I'm going to ask her out the same day as another girl. Is that really worth—whatever it is I think I'm doing? I stand there for a moment, dazed, before I remember that I'm supposed to be meeting Charlotte here. I look down the hallway in both directions but see no one, so I whip out my phone and text her.

Where are you?

She takes a moment to reply.

You're a dolt

My heart sinks. She must have seen me ask out Miracle Girl. I thought I'd made it clear I was joking yesterday with the pickup line thing, but she obviously wasn't. I actually physically facepalm since there's no one

44

around to see me. Way to go, Levi. I should probably try to make it up to her somehow. Then I remember that I still don't have Miracle Girl's name or number. She'd better be there on Thursday, or else I'll be back to square one.

* * *

Over the next two days I text Charlotte on and off. To my surprise, she doesn't totally ignore me. She's slightly colder to me than she was before, though, and when I try to apologize directly, she replies with a tombstone emoji that I have no idea how to interpret.

Thursday at seven finds me waiting next to a light pole illuminating the giant statue of a mammoth on the south end of campus. I can't seem to stop my fingers from drumming on the concrete base that the light pole sits on, but other than that, I'm not feeling too nervous. I'm not sure what taking Mystery Girl on a date is supposed to do for her, or how it's supposed to help me understand the light I saw inside her before. I just know that if I don't do something, she's going to have to carry her back-breaking load alone. I'm not okay with that. I'll just have to go with the flow tonight and see what happens.

I resist the urge to check my watch again to see how much time has gone by. It was fifteen minutes past the time she said she'd be here the last time I looked. I let out a breath. I shouldn't have gotten my hopes up.

"Hey."

I turn, and there she is, swathed in darkness. The radiant glow from the streetlight falls like a halo to the crown of her head, cascading from there down every strand of hair and splaying off with glowing tendrils into the night, making her profile shine with an ethereal aura. For a split second, even though she's literally right in front of me, she looks so much like a character from some

45

kind of fantasy novel that I have a hard time believing that she's actually real.

She smiles at me, and it's a lot warmer than I was expecting.

"You actually look happy to see me," I notice with some surprise.

"Don't let it go to your head."

Something about the remark feels...familiar somehow.

"I wouldn't dream of it."

As one, we turn and head towards the art building.

"Sorry I'm late. The only time I could get a practice room today was right before this, and I lost track of time."

"Practice room for what?"

Presumably something related to that enormous collection of sheet music she has.

"For...just...stuff."

"Hmm."

"Don't look at me like that. It's nothing shady."

"Sure."

When she reaches for the door, I notice a slight tremble to her hand.

"Wait, are you nervous?"

She gives me a death glare.

"Don't be. I'm not that exciting."

"Well, that's for sure."

Inside, we approach the ticket counter. Miracle Girl looks at the price and stops cold. Her hand drifts hesitantly toward her wallet.

"I've got it."

She relaxes a little, but she's still awfully tense.

"Hey, chill. I already think you're great, so no pressure."

She gives me a look that I can't interpret. I hand over my credit card, and we go in. We kind of wander around a bit. There's a number of people around, but the exhibition is broken up into a variety of rooms, and there are few enough in any one place that I'm not as uncomfortable as I'd normally be in a place like this. Miracle Girl doesn't seem all that interested in the actual artwork. To be honest, I'm not either.

"I haven't seen you at the library."

"What's it to you?"

"I hope I didn't scare you off."

She shrugs.

"It'd take a lot more than that."

"That's good. How's...your mental health?"

There's no way to phrase it that doesn't feel incredibly awkward.

"I'm not that fragile."

"Good. Sorry. I'm a bit more familiar with the medical side, if I'm being honest."

"Premed?"

"Yeah."

"I wouldn't have pegged you as the type to pry open people's innards."

"No? I am pretty good at prying into other people's affairs. I mean, I did just ask a complete stranger on a date." As I say this my mind brushes over Micah's comment about the White Knight Complex, and I flinch a little inside. We wander into the next room. It's full of pictures of bowls of fruit. We share a glance and walk right back out.

"That's only an issue if the stranger doesn't want you to pry," she says finally. I look at her. For the briefest of moments, I catch a glimpse of the spark I saw before.

"You seem awfully...lonely." I realize the words are true the moment they leave my lips.

"Well you seem very--" She pokes around half-heartedly for a comeback and then gives up.

"Unexceptional," I provide.

"Yes, now that you mention it. Kind of." She looks at me in a penetrating way that makes me want to hide in a corner.

"I'm a singer," she says out of nowhere.

"What?"

"You asked me what I use the practice room for. That's it. I sing." Her voice trembles ever so slightly.

"That's nothing to be ashamed of."

"I'm *not* ashamed of it!"

She says it with such intensity that I actually physically back up a step.

"I just don't like people knowing about it," she continues.

"Why not?"

"Because if people didn't get why it's so important to me, I wouldn't be able to handle it."

"And you think I do?"

"I think you're less likely to mess it up than average."

"Thanks. I think."

She won't look at me. Her shoulders are hunched up so far I'm worried that she'll herniate a disk.

"I can't say that I totally understand," I say. "But I'd like to."

"Okay."

"Really? No snarky comment? No screaming at me to get out of your life?"

Her eyes dance all over my forehead before averting once more.

"Maybe I'm just too tired to fight it."

I feel bad for her. Suddenly something clicks.

"You're Charlotte, aren't you?" A smile flicks across her lips before she can stop it.

"It's about time you figured it out. I thought for sure you were as dense as a can of bricks after you had a full conversation with me without realizing it."

"Can of bricks?"

"Shut up."

"So that's why you got all mad at me!"

"You really are such a dolt." She peels the mask off her face and tosses it in a nearby trashcan, making me even more curious about why she was wearing it in the first place.

"Hey! It's hard to recognize someone when they're wearing one of those. Also, why were your eyes brown?"

Suddenly a switch flips and she shuts down.

"Sorry, you don't have to--"

"It's okay," she says in a tone of voice that tells me it's not. Luckily, we're in a somewhat secluded part of the exhibit, so there aren't many people around to interrupt. It hits me how easy it's been to talk to her compared to most of the human race. It's taken this long for the conversation to ground to a halt for the first time.

"I won't ask again." I tell her. Time to change the subject. "So, uh, who's your team?"

"I hate sports."

"Oh. Yeah, I'll watch 'em, but I'm not super hardcore," I pivot wildly. "Uh, what kind of music are you into?"

"I hate it."

"You're a singer who hates music?"

She turns away from me.

"I touched a nerve, and now you hate everything."

"Pretty much."

I nod slowly.

"So, uh, what do I do now?"

"Just hug me."

After a small internal battle, I close the distance and pull her in. She slaps my arm and tries to shrink away halfheartedly but quickly drops the act and leans into me. Her breath goes all long and deep like a puppy lapping up ice cold water on a hot day. I feel a little weird about it, but at least she's not pushing me away anymore.

"My parents want me to quit singing," she whispers.
"Why?"
"So I can focus more on school."
"Do *you* want to?"
She shakes her head.
"Then don't."
"Okay."
"I'll help you."
Nod.
"Okay."

We stand in silence. I think about how much it must suck to have everyone in your life trying to convince you to give up the thing that you love the most.

Finally Charlotte pulls away, but it's not the halfhearted turtle-shell pull she tried a minute ago. She reaches for my hand, but I somehow manage to pull it away without turning it into a rejection. Then I hear a voice. One of my least favorite voices in the world and the absolute last one I would ever want to hear in this situation. If you don't know who it is from that, I obviously haven't stressed enough how much I hate my roommate's freaking guts.

Chapter 7

I step forward and instinctively put myself in front of Charlotte to shield her from the oncoming onslaught.

"What are you doing here, Micah?" I ask with as much venom as I can muster.

"I'm here for an assignment." His smirk is more subtle than usual, but somehow that makes it all the more insufferable. See, it isn't a coincidence that he's here right now. I told him I was going on a date to the art exhibit, but I never dreamed in a million years that he would deliberately crash it. Even just his presence here makes me feel like an insect he's peeling the wings off of.

His eyes flick up to Charlotte's and the smirk widens ever so minutely. He knows who she is. I realize too late that my protective maneuver only made it more obvious that there's something here for him to stick his nose into. I swear, if he tries to pull Charlotte into one of his soul-sucking arguments I *will give him a FREAKING knuckle sandwich.* I start walking her toward the exit. I want to avoid talking as much as possible to limit the number traps he can lure me into, but I can't help but challenge his alibi as I prep our escape.

"You're at an art exhibition for a philosophy class?"

"Not all of my classes are philosophy, Levi. I'm taking an art history class for one of my generals. But actually art *does* have a lot of overlap with philosophy because artists also tend to think about the big questions."

I will not be baited. I will not be baited. I will not be baited! Only a few feet to go, and we're out of here. I'm not even going to try to be polite about it.

"I'm surprised you made it this far into the exhibit without engaging a few of the paintings in a debate about the existence of the universe or something."

"It's much more interesting to see such things in action." His eyes jump to Charlotte again, and I wish I had a way to stop them. We're at the threshold to the next room. Just a few more steps. He continues, "Especially the way people try so hard to cover up their *animal instincts.*"

I stop.

"Are you kidding me right now?!" I abruptly realize how deep the months upon months of angst toward him runs as it all gushes to the surface in a single, sudden surge.

"Do you seriously have to ruin EVERY SINGLE THING that is beautiful in this world? Can't you JUST ONCE leave me be when something is going well for me? What good is all your philosophy when it just makes life worse the more you talk about it? I'm SICK of it."

To my horror, Micah's smirk widens to a full-on grin.

"When you get angry in an argument," he says quietly, "it means that you've lost but aren't willing to admit it."

I whirl around and storm away, fully aware as I do so that it is only cementing my defeat even further. Even worse, I can feel Charlotte start to tense up again. The very moment she started to trust me enough to let me in, I had to go and kick it in the teeth. And the very, very worst part is that it's not all Micah's fault. I'm the one who let him get to me. By the time we get to the entrance of the building, I'm so disappointed in myself I can't see straight.

"I'm sorry you had to see that," I say. "I really suck sometimes."

"I'm glad," Charlotte says quietly. "If you were perfect, I'd be too intimidated to be around you. Don't worry, there's never been any risk of that. You didn't even take my advice to make sure I liked art before you asked me here."

"Ouch. I think. Wait, *do* you like art?"

"It's okay."

The heat of my anger ticks down a couple of degrees.

"See you around," she says. For the first time she actually seems to mean it. We part ways, and I circle back toward my apartment, walking quickly. If I can get there fast enough, I can be sleeping by the time Micah gets back. At the very thought, I speed up even more. It's only four blocks, but the thought of Micah chasing me down and yanking me back into our previous conversation makes it feel like a light year.

The apartment is in sight when I suddenly realize that someone is walking beside me. I let out a little yelp and almost jump out of my skin, ready to sprint at the sight of Micah's oily black hair.

"Fancy seeing you here, Levi."

It's Mason. My heart rate drops by half. I force myself to slow down a little to be polite.

"Hey. You don't have to force yourself to chat with me. I can see you've got a lot on your mind." Ironically it's probably the only thing he could have said that makes me actually want to spill. Man, he's good.

"I'm just really mad at myself."

"Most people are."

"I don't know if I'm going to be able to help the person I told you about last time."

Somehow I'm expecting this to turn into an intense heart-to-heart like before, but instead Mason just says, "You'll figure it out," pats me on the shoulder, hops into his car at the edge of the apartment complex parking lot, and drives off. Somehow it's the perfect thing.

I let myself breathe a little. I'm still frustrated. At the same time, even though I'm not about to stay up waiting for Micah to get back, I'm not as afraid of running into him as I was a second ago. My date with Charlotte wasn't really a win or a loss. It was just a messy bundle of things that you can't really slap a single label on. I did my best, and I guess that's what matters.

As I head up the walk to my apartment, I haven't the faintest idea the immeasurable impact the last couple of hours is going to have on the rest of my life. In fact, it's a good thing that I don't know at this point. If I knew this instant what's just around the corner for me, it would scare me spitless. My life as I know it is about to change.

Chapter 8

The next morning I wake up as early as humanly possible and jet out the door before the crack of dawn. There's already a text on my phone from Charlotte. I chuckle a little as I read it.

I hate you less every day.

I can't help but smile as I tap out a quick reply:

Good morning to you, too.

That's progress, for sure. I'm still not sure how exactly I'm supposed to make things better for her; I just know that I want to. The desire burns brightly in my chest, growing ever brighter as the days pass. We hang out a few times over the next couple of weeks. Nothing too intense, just mostly doing homework in the same vicinity, and such like. It doesn't take long for me to sense that something is seriously wrong.

The first hint comes when I invite Charlotte to grab lunch a couple of days after the date at the art gallery.

"Uh, no," she says, trying to hide behind her hair.

"All right."

I'm used to those types of responses from her, so at first I don't think much of it. But then she turns me down again the next night for dinner, as well as for lunch two days later. She's perfectly willing take a walk around campus or catch one of the free concerts the School of Music is always putting on, but eating out is some reason off limits.

At first I think she's got some weird food thing going on, but then she says no to hitting the movies on Friday, and again when I invite her to a basketball game.

"What's going on, Char?" I ask the next time she tells me no. "Are you allergic to having fun or something?"

"No, just to you."

"But you're with me all the time."

"Exactly. I'm up to my ears in Benadryl."

"Seriously, what's going on? You know I'm not going to judge you for it. I just want to know why you cop out on me randomly."

She turns away from me, which tells me I might actually get a real answer.

"To be honest, I haven't really gotten the whole pulling-money-out-of-my-hair thing down."

"You're broke."

"Don't rub it in!"

"So broke that you can't buy a three-dollar burger?"

She still can't look at me.

"You're serious. You really can't afford it? What are you eating?"

The edge of her face, which is all I can see from this angle, is turning pink.

"Sorry, I didn't mean to make you feel weird about it."

"Well you're doing an awful job."

"Sorry."

"No, you're not."

"Wait a minute!" Something has just clicked. "That's why you haven't been driving to school lately. Because you don't have enough money to get your tire fixed, and you're scared of getting another flat while using your spare."

She doesn't look at me. I fish around in my wallet for a twenty, which I try to hand to her. She stares down at it. Her unpainted nails brush over the bill, but she doesn't take it.

"What's wrong?"

"Do you have any idea," she says slowly, "how much this sucks?"

My hand freezes.

"No. I don't."

"I don't take handouts."

"Why not?"

"Because this is a me problem."

"A you problem."

"Yes. I want to pay my own way."

That makes sense. Now that I think about it, she *did* look fairly uncomfortable when we were trying to decide who was going to pay for the art exhibit the other day. She doesn't want to go places that cost money because she'll have to mooch off of other people. However--

"It's not like I'm paying my own way either. Most of my money comes from my dad. There's no shame in using some of it for a good cause. This way you won't have to walk through that sketchy area around your apartment every time you go in or out."

Her eyes narrow at the word "sketchy." I probably should have phrased that differently.

"I'll pass."

"Or if you don't want to use it on the tire, you could at least get yourself something to eat."

Her stomach rumbles like it's home to a live rhinoceros. I hand the twenty to her again, and she takes it. She turns to go.

"It's not a 'you' problem if I'm in it with you," I say.

She stops but doesn't turn around, staring numbly at the money in her hand.

"Just a thought."

* * *

For some reason, the more time I spend with Charlotte, the less my life feels like the endless pit of drudgery that it normally does. I'm not entirely sure why. It's not like she's particularly perky, or that I've been all that successful in helping her. But for the first time since I can remember, the clouds have parted.

Lindsay lets out a low whimper next to me, and I realize that I've been spacing out thinking about that conversation with Charlotte from a couple of days ago. I hope I didn't miss anything important.

"I swear," she says with all the feeling of her whole soul, "if she throws us *one* more curve ball, I'm going to...I don't know. Give her a nasty review online."

"If so, we'll figure it out."

"Aren't you a bundle of sunshine this morning?"

"Always."

Actually that isn't at all true, but today I am, at least more than usual.

There's another text on from Charlotte on my phone when I leave class.

Want to do lunch?

Oh we're doing that now, are we? I can't help but smile because I see it as a clear sign of progress. I'm actually a pretty big cheapskate with most things. In fact I usually don't even buy food on campus when I can avoid it. Today it feels a lot more worth it, though, because at least I can guarantee that Charlotte gets one decent meal. My stomach turns at the thought because it reminds me of all the days she almost certainly *hasn't* gotten one. Isn't there scholarship money out there for stuff like this?

Charlotte has on slightly more makeup today than normal and is looking a little distracted. She's already sitting at a table when I get to the food court. The gloom I'd been feeling about her money issues dissipates for the most part as I see her.

"Hey!"

She looks up and kind of grimaces slightly.

"What do you want to eat?" I ask.

"Eh—whatever you want."

"Are you okay?"

"Swell."

"No really, what's up?"

"It's nothing." I give her the most skeptical look I can manage.

"Well, then I'm buying." With no further input incoming, I head over to the Greek fast food place and buy a couple gyros. When I get back, Charlotte is looking a little perkier. She doesn't say anything about the gyros, but stops morosely staring off into space, which I take as an endorsement. She opens hers and slowly starts picking off the tomatoes.

"Sorry I should have asked first."

"Yeah, you should have" she says with a smile she can't quite hide, and suddenly the world is back in its usual orbit.

"Does your roommate ever chill?" she asks me.

It takes me a second to realize she must be talking about Micah's date-crashing tendencies.

"I don't really know. There are times when he's a bit less abrasive, I guess, but I don't think I've ever seen him not be...'nihilistic' is his word for it. Like he has a vendetta against anything that could possibly cheer people up. I haven't seen him recently, though. I've been trying to stay as far away from him as possible since—you know."

"Smart." Silence creeps in again, but there isn't as much pressure to fill it as there sometimes is.

"What are your parents like?" I land on finally.

"They have about as much rizz as moldy cabbage," she says fondly. There's still a bit of edge to her voice, but it's impossible to tell if it's due to her mood or the subject matter. "They like to nose into all of my business."

"Huh. That's hard for me to imagine."

"What is?"

"Parents who actually talk to you regularly."

"What?" Charlotte smacks her gyro wrapper with an open hand. The girl at the next table glares at us, but we ignore her.

"I mean, I do *talk* to my dad, but he normally just goes on and on about money."

"Rude."

"I know, right?"

"Lamers gotta lame." A bulky guy sits down at the next table as well, talking animatedly. Charlotte tucks her head down slightly.

"What's wrong?"

"Nothing," she says, fully aware that I know she's lying.

There's pain in her eyes. It's always there, actually, but sometimes it bubbles to the surface more fully than others. I've learned that she's a lot more likely to open up on her own if I don't push it.

"All right, then."

Now it's her turn to go for a subject change.

"Do you dance?"

"*Dance?*"

"You know, swirl people around and all that."

"Why?"

Her face looks the way mine probably does when I've just stuffed my foot into my mouth and it's too late to back out.

"I'm, ah, part of the Swing Dance Club. They might have me sing a couple of numbers at the end of club next week. If the right people see it and I land something bigger, maybe I can get my parents to rethink making me quit. But if you don't really--"

"Yeah, I'll come."

"Really?"

"Don't sound so surprised. If anything, I'm shocked you're willing to risk your toes with me."

She shrugs.

"If I'm going to get them trodden on, I'd rather do it with you than some--" she eyes the bulky guy, who's begun to raise his voice a little bit-- "bozo."

She lets out a little breath that I probably wasn't supposed to hear and pulls her chair a little farther away from the argument next to us.

"You don't think I'm a bozo, huh?"

"Yeah, but you're a lovable one so it doesn't count."

Suddenly the guy, who I've surmised from what he's been yelling about is the boyfriend of Annoyed Girl, jumps to his feet.

"Why is it always my fault? You NEVER take responsibility. I am DONE with this."

Charlotte pulls as far away as she can get from them on her chair. She's gone as white as a sheet, and her shoulders are shaking so hard I can see it from across the table. She's breathing like a machine gun, each gulp of air coming in and out rapid fire.

"Charlotte?"

Her eyes are totally void of all comprehension. She's a mouse staring down a particularly hungry mountain lion.

"If you can't trust me not to cheat on you, I don't know what to say to you!" Bozo points at his girlfriend threateningly. He's obviously upset, but I'm not really getting violent vibes from him, so I'm totally nonplussed by Charlotte's reaction. Then it hits me: Whatever went down in the library is happening all over again. I'm suddenly on the receiving end of a ginormous spike of fear. What exactly am I supposed to do? I stand up and walk around to her side of the table, but she shrinks away from me too. I look on helplessly.

"Well, if you're so innocent, why won't you let me see your phone?" says Girlfriend.

This doesn't look like it's going to end anytime soon, so I reach for Charlotte's arm again. This time she lets me take it. I scoop up our half-eaten gyros and make a beeline for the exit. The couple is so engrossed in their fight that they don't even notice.

Charlotte sags into me a little bit. Her heart is pounding like a jackrabbit on Red Bull. It's making me almost as scared as she is. This won't hurt her, will it? I lead her down a couple of random hallways and sit her down on a bench.

"Are you okay? Should I try to find those counselors again?"

Her violet eyes, now full of terror, stare back at me, still uncomprehending.

"It's okay, Charlotte. They're gone." No response.

"Look at me." Her head turns slowly toward me.

"It's safe now." Those words seem to accomplish something because she blinks slowly, and her eyes refocus a bit. I reach toward her again, and she recoils like I'm a snake.

"Sorry," she says. "I'm sorry." Tears peek over the edges of her eyelids.

"Sorry? I'm the one who was--"

"I'm sorry. I'm sorry. I'm sorry." She slowly stands. I'm a bit afraid she'll take off running, but there's nothing I can do to stop her that won't make her even more skittish. Now the tears really come, running rivers down her cheeks. Her breathing has slowed somewhat and now comes in huge, seizing gasps. I wait. Eventually she leans against the wall a little and seems to pull herself together somewhat.

"What was that?" I ask.

"Nothing you need to worry about."

"I'm sorry," it's my turn to say, although I don't really know what I'm apologizing for.

"You should be." It's funny how that's the phrase that tells me she's okay again. Well, mostly.

"Are you going to be okay singing tomorrow night?"

"There are a lot of people who sign up for the live music spots. If I don't take them, someone else will."

"And that's worth risking your health?"

"Yes."

There's something in her expression that makes me believe her. Well, if it's important enough to her to take the chance that something like this will happen again, it's important to me too.

"But Charlotte, what if something like this happens in the middle of your performance?"

She looks up at me.

"That's why I need you there."

Chapter 9

The way Charlotte explains it, the worst part of those—attacks, or whatever they are, is the anticipation.

"It can happen at any moment. I never know when it's coming."

"That sounds *awful*."

"Pretty much. And if I'm already feeling anxious about something, it's even more likely."

"So if you're feeling nervous for the performance--"

"Exactly. And I really, *really* don't want it to happen somewhere I can't get away."

"What would happen if you couldn't?"

"I don't know. Nothing. Everything. I know I shouldn't feel that way about it, but my dumb brain doesn't seem to believe me."

"It's not dumb."

She gives me a skeptical look.

"It isn't. Look, you didn't choose any of this, right?"

"...No."

"So stop blaming yourself. The way you feel about this makes sense."

"Does it?" she asks with a certain iciness.

"Well, I mean, I've never felt that way personally, but I can picture it. And you don't have to do this by yourself. I'll be there, too. It'll be okay."

Charlotte's jaw tightens. She doesn't seem completely convinced.

"There's one thing I still don't understand, though. How does me being at your performance help with any of that?"

"Because you feel...safe." The last word forces its way out of her painfully, as if squeezed from a nearly depleted tube of toothpaste. My heart warms as she says it.

"So I'm like a rescue helicopter waiting in the wings to swoop in and whisk you away if your house catches on fire."

"If rescue helicopters flew right past their targets when they're wearing different colored contacts."

"Ouch. You're never going to let me live that down, are you?"

"Nope. Yeah, that's basically it, though. If I know there's a way out, it's a lot less likely to hit me in the first place."

I nod.

"I'll be there. You can count on it."

* * *

The day before Swing Dance Club I meet with my O-chem project group. We're all a bit frazzled. Balancing work on the end-of-term project with the weekly assignments has been difficult. On top of that, research for the paper is proving to be more challenging than expected.

"Why on earth is it so hard to find research papers on specific elimination reactions?" groans Raymond, clutching his head in his hands.

"There probably are some," I say. "The problem is that they were all done in the early 1900's, and the professor wants more modern research."

"Should we pivot then?" suggests Lindsay. "What elimination reactions does the more modern research care about?"

"Well, there's a bunch of stuff on obscure subatomic particles. But that goes beyond the scope of this class. There are also a few studies on achieving E1 reactions on very heavy elements, but a lot of these are extreme cases using specialized equipment."

"Is there an AI tool that can comb the databases for us? As long it's not actually writing the paper for us, it should be okay, right?"

"I don't think we have time to be finicky," adds Raymond. "Even if we got all our research by tonight, getting it all written by tomorrow would still be tight."

Wait.

"What do you mean tomorrow?" I ask. "We're not even halfway through the semester yet."

"Did you see the message the professor put out on MammothLearn last week?" says Lindsay.

"No..."

"She's making the paper the midterm. The final is just the presentation."

"With *one week's notice*?"

"That's why I was so upset in class last time."

I groaned inwardly. How had I missed that?

"When's it due?"

"Tomorrow at midnight," says Raymond. "We've gotta meet tomorrow afternoon and grind it out until the deadline."

Tomorrow afternoon. That's right during Swing Dance Club.

"Can we do it today instead?"

Raymond shakes his head.

"No can do. I have an exam later."

"What about earlier in the day tomorrow?"

"I'll be at work all day," says Lindsay.

"I have a conflict tomorrow afternoon," I admit.

Lindsay groans.

"What kind of conflict?" asks Raymond.

"A friend of mine is singing at Swing Dance Club."

Raymond's eyes narrow.

"I get that you want to be there, but not failing O-Chem is a heck of a lot more important."

"It's not just that. She has some mental health stuff going on, so--"

"What stuff?" asks Lindsay.

"I'm...not sure exactly. But it will be a lot harder for her if I don't go."

"What, you're her emotional support animal or something?" said Raymond. "I'm sure she can get by without you just fine for one night."

I grind my teeth in frustration. It's not like I don't know where he's coming from. If I hadn't seen one of Charlotte's attacks firsthand, I wouldn't have understood either. Still, was he seriously not even going to *try* to get it?

"I *have* to be there."

"Well maybe you can find another group, then."

"There isn't time for that," said Lindsay. "And Dr. Sato isn't going to let us switch teams anyway. We can figure this out, guys. Come on."

I groan inwardly. We're in big trouble here. If we don't get that paper submitted tomorrow, our grades are going to tank, and any chance at medical school will go up in smoke. On the other hand, there's no way I'm going to let Charlotte down right as she's started to trust me.

"Why did we even wait this long to start on it?" I complain. "We should have taken care of it earlier."

"That's not going to help us now," says Lindsay. "I think we're going to have to grab whatever sources are most relevant and just make them fit somehow. We can meet at my apartment, since we're going to have to go pretty late."

"You're still going to meet tomorrow?"

"*We're* going to meet tomorrow," says Raymond.

We stare each other down. I can feel my temperature start to rise. Then something dawns on me. There is exactly one course of action that lets me have it all: doing it everything myself. Is it even possible? This could be cutting it close. I take a deep breath.

"All right, guys. I'm going go to get a head start on the research for tomorrow."

"Sounds good," says Lindsay.

"Ten four, dude," says Raymond, relaxing a little.

I leave the building at a speedwalk. The library is only a couple of hundred yards from the science building, but I'm already breathing heavily as I reach the entrance. The first floor is mostly open area, so I sprint up the stairs to the second. I settle down at a cubicle-like desk by the periodical section, far enough away from the main thoroughfare to have privacy, but close enough not to have to spend much time getting there. I whip out my laptop and boot it up. It's time to grind. Luckily, I'm done with class for the day, and I have just one quick assignment due for Biology tomorrow. I hammer it out as quickly as I can and open the school's scientific journal database.

I had been looking for sources for the project just yesterday, but there's a new urgency to my search today. I want Charlotte to have a performance she can be proud of without worrying about more mental health stuff cropping up. The only way that's going to happen is if I'm there tomorrow. I'm not going to let anything stand in my way, not even Chemistry Purgatory itself.

It takes me an hour and a half to get enough sources for my part of the project. That's not bad at all, but it's still just one-third of what we need. Next is Lindsay's piece. She's not going to like me doing it for her, but she'll probably get over it. Hers ends up being a little trickier, but after two hours of deep struggle, I find what I'm looking for in an obscure journal on biological chemistry. Two down. I'm getting hungry now, but I don't dare stop to eat yet. Now it's time for Raymond's part.

At first I'm feeling optimistic because I'm still on pace to finish while the night is still relatively young, but soon I realize that this is going to be harder than I had anticipated. There isn't really any of the current E1 reaction research that will work for our project. Sure, they're mentioned, but there isn't anything that talks about their practical application in real life, which is something we need for the paper. I start avoiding looking at the clock as the minutes tick away. How can there be nothing? Surely E1 reactions matter for things other than O-Chem professor job security. I'm starting to get discouraged, and my mind is getting cloudy from hunger and from staying focused for so long.

Take a break, my mind tells me. *Just ten minutes. Look at social media for a bit.* Most days that would be all it took to get me off track, but this isn't most days.

Suddenly something clicks. What if instead of searching for articles about E1 directly, I look up studies about methods of boosting SN1 reactions, since they so often compete with E1? With another deep breath, I wade into the fray again. I'm starting to find articles that are closer to something we could use. Isn't there a study somewhere about maximizing SN1 reactions? I click on the next article.

There it is. THE EFFICACY OF ETHEL GROUP SUBSTRATES AS A FACILITATOR OF SN1 REACTIONS. Hallelujah! I use the literature review section of the article to immediately find three more studies that these authors cited. Done. Time for a break to grab some food before I start writing it. I finally allow myself to look at the clock and immediately wince. It's 10 PM. Then I see the notification on my phone. It's a missed call. With a touch of a finger I pull up more details and see that it's from Charlotte. I pack up my stuff and head out into the common area to call her back.

Ring. Ring. Ring.

"Hello?"

"Hey, Charlotte. What's up?"

"Oh, nothing."

"I saw that you called."

"What's it to you?"

"Just happy to hear from you."

"As if." She seems to have shaken off whatever it was that was affecting her the other day.

"So what's up?"

"Oh, nothing."

Huh?

"No, seriously, what is it?"

"I wanted to see if you were hungry, but--"

"Yeah, for sure!" I chime in before she can back out. "Where are you?"

* * *

Ten minutes later I find myself in front of Charlotte's apartment. I'm a little confused about what's going on with her today. She sounds mostly normal, but there is something just slightly reticent about voice, like she is reluctant to talk to me. At the same time, she's the one who called me. What exactly is going through her head right now?

I feel a little weird about walking here at this time of night, but Charlotte had assured me it was fine.

"Stay in lit areas. Keep your head down. Don't poke your nose anywhere it doesn't belong. You should be fine," she'd said. Very specific advice. Almost like she knows it from experience.

I knock on the door. It's pitch black inside her apartment, so she's probably back in her room. The apartment complex is fairly small, just eight units in two blocks of four with two units parked atop two others twice. Luckily Charlotte's is on the bottom and fairly easy to find. The parking lot is pitch black save for a single dim light above each apartment door, which only makes me more nervous. How was I supposed to stay in lit areas when there *were* no lit areas?

Charlotte still hasn't answered. Frowning, I knock again, then whip out my phone again and text her.

Where are you?

This is getting weirder by the second. Did she fall asleep on me, or something? Finally the door opens, but the front room is so dark that it takes me a second to realize that it is indeed Charlotte.

"You took your sweet time," I tease. Unexpectedly, she doesn't poke back at me.

"Yeah, sorry." Something is a bit off about her, but it's hard to tell what.

"Look, I don't think I can do this tonight," she says.

"That's chill, but...are you okay?"

She takes far too long to respond.

"Yeah."

"Baloney."

She sighs.

"Yeah."

"So what's up?"

"I can't tell you."

"Why not?"

"Because not."

"What does that even mean?

"I just can't!"

"All right, sorry."

"Me too."

Was it really a good idea for her to be trying to sing tomorrow like this? What if she has another attack and it causes a medical problem or something? Does that happen? On the other hand, she's determined enough to see this through that I'm not going to be able to stop her. There's part of me that admires that, to be honest. What is it about singing that's so important to her that she's willing to take this kind of risk?

"See you at Swing Dance tomorrow," she says.

I almost tell her there's some risk that I won't be there, but I just can't. There is no "if." I *will* be there, no matter what.

"Yeah, I'm looking forward to it."

"Good."

Deep breath. I can do this.

"Sorry."

She grabs my wrist.

"Don't be sorry." I can't see her face, but there's a slight shakiness to her voice. "Don't be sorry. I just suck."

I slowly pull my hand away.

"No, you don't. Everyone has a secret or two."

The dark outline of her silhouette shifts back and forth as she shakes her head silently.

"Not like mine."

* * *

My detour to Charlotte's apartment and back takes me a total of about a half hour, making it 10:30 PM when I get back to the library. I still haven't eaten anything, but there's no time for that now. I've got to make sure to get enough of the paper done that my group doesn't hate me for leaving early tomorrow. Fortunately, since we've had some discussion about the project already, I have a pretty clear direction for the paper. I start writing. The introduction is fairly straightforward; I lay out my thesis statement and the main points of the paper without missing a beat. Then I start on the first body paragraph. This is where the grind really starts. I pull up the rubric, which enumerates no less than fifteen elements I need to cover in each of the three sections.

Here we go.

It's getting late enough now that my efficiency is starting to drop a little. It's taking more effort to stay focused. Enough words are making it onto the paper still that I'm not too worried yet, but that may not hold true for long. I realize one of the sources I grabbed won't actually work with the way my argument is developing, but luckily it's for the section that's easier to research for. Ten more minutes, and I'm back on track again. All right, on to section two. My focus is starting to slip to the point that I have to keep pulling myself back to the task at hand. I keep thinking about the way Charlotte's voice was quivering earlier. Why did she go to all the trouble of calling me only to cancel? And why did she want to get something to eat at ten at night? There's something strange about all of this.

Abruptly, I realize I've been staring off into space and force my eyes back to my laptop. Okay, on to how E2 reactions deal with proton donors. I buckle down again. Just a few minutes later, however, the library is suddenly filled with music. I sigh. No, the orchestra isn't doing an impromptu performance in the middle of the night. The library's closing. I'm going to have to relocate. As I pack up for home, I realize that an unintentional side benefit of my plan is that I've successfully avoided Micah all day. On a whim I text Charlotte.

You aren't getting sick, are you?

That would explain a lot. As soon as I hit send I remember that it's literally one in the morning. Oops. When I reach the bottom floor, my pocket vibrates. She's actually responded.

Not as sick as you are

It's a pretty normal answer from her, but I'm getting suspicious that I may have underestimated the extent to which she's been covering up her level of struggle. Especially since she texted me back in the middle of the night on a weekday.

I try to walk home quickly to save time, but I'm starting to reach the limit of how hard I can push myself. My brain feels like a lump of dough, and it's taking twice the time to process each thought.

After about an eternity, I make it back to the apartment. Blissfully, there's no Micah, as predicted. There is, however, Mason. He's been home a lot more often lately, I notice.

"Late night," he comments.

"Not as late as it's going to be," I reply, choosing the least comfortable chair in the kitchen so as to better keep myself awake.

"Well, good luck." He's halfway into his bedroom when I remember that this is the one person in my world who might know something about what happened to Charlotte this morning.

"Hey, quick question. Can someone get a heart attack from anxiety?"

He stops.

"This about you, or someone you know?"

I wonder if he somehow already guesses who it is.

"Someone I know."

"What happened?"

"The other day we were eating lunch when the couple next to us started fighting and she just—shut down. Got all pale and her pulse was really, really high."

Mason nods. "Was the couple yelling at each other by chance?"

"They were going at it like a couple of wild beasts."

"Could be a panic attack. Do you know if the person has had anything traumatic happen to her involving people yelling?"

"Not that I know of, but I really don't know that much about her."

"Panic attacks are often triggered by running into something that reminds you of your past trauma. They can be incredibly frightening for the one experiencing them, but they aren't dangerous. It could also be a flashback, which is when a person checks out of reality and feels like they're experiencing their trauma all over again. Again, we don't want her to go through that more than she has to, but it's not going to cause some kind of medical incident."

I don't understand how he can be nonchalant about something so intense, but I guess he does do this for a living. It's good to know that panic attacks aren't going to hurt her, though. That's one less thing for me to worry about for tomorrow.

"I'm not sure I get the difference. What if it's both a panic attack *and* a flashback?"

"It could be. Or even something in between. These categories are not as clear-cut as sometimes they seem."

"Okay, thanks,".

"Sure. Anytime." He disappears back into his room.

Well, I'm awake now, but not in a way that's helpful for essay writing. The thought that I might have to help Charlotte with something I barely understand has me wired. I set up shop again, but even though I'm more alert, it's even harder to focus than before. Are panic attacks permanent? What if I do something to set her off? Or what if I make it worse somehow?

Stop it. Focus. One step at a time. She is starting to turn to me for support, so that's got to mean something, right? I'm suddenly profoundly grateful that Micah is asleep again so he can't sow more self-doubt. Oh no, I've gotten distracted again. Focus! Essay!

I start writing again. It's the only thing I can do for Charlotte right now, so I'd better focus on it. I wrap up my thoughts on E1 reactions and start on the next section.

As the night wears on, I slowly grow more lucid, although I know from experience that tomorrow morning will be an entirely different story. I don't actually have to finish the whole essay right now. I just need to do enough that my group members feel good about the timeline. My plan is to get enough of the E2 section done to make it clear the direction I'm heading with it. Okay, let's check the rubric again.

Discuss each type of reaction...use sources to support your arguments...relate each reaction to the core principles of Organic Chemistry. My heart drops out of my chest. I completely missed that. I go back to section one and start working again with a growing sense of dread. Am I even going to be able to function tomorrow? There's no time to think about that. The more time I spend worrying, the less I'll spend sleeping.

I slowly work my way through the first section again, adding the elements I missed the first time around. I'm not doing a particularly good job. Hopefully my group members will see it as a solid rough draft and give me a pass. It takes me much longer than it should to finish, but finally I wrap up that part and move on to section two. I'm almost there! Just a little further.

I open my eyes without any memory of having closed them. My head is pounding and my neck is aching. How long was I out? Panicked, I plunge my hand into my pocket and whip out my phone. It's 2:45 AM. Whew. I can deal with that. Then I see the other notification. Charlotte texted half an hour ago.

Can we talk?

I head outside in search of privacy. The outside air is crisp and cool, which is nice. It helps my head stop spinning quite as fast. My mind is pretty well mush right now, but enough of is still functioning to feel increasingly worried. Seriously, what's up, Charlotte? Well, I'll know in a second. I hit dial.

No answer. Ugh, seriously? Dejected, I head back inside, worry gnawing at me like a swarm of particularly ravenous termites. It's just as well that I have more to get done on the essay. I wouldn't be able to sleep right now anyway.

It's fine. I'll just talk to her tomorrow. I start into section two a second time. If I can get that completely finished, it should be enough to be done for tonight. My progress is at a crawl right now. Between the headache, the mental fog, and worrying about Charlotte, it's all I can do to string two words together. I keep glancing back at the rubric to keep me focused. I'm almost there.

At long last, section two is finished. I slam my laptop shut and hurl myself into bed without even bothering to change out of my clothes. My stomach is absolutely snarling at me, but there's no way I'm going to prioritize food over rest at this point. It takes painfully long for me to drift away into oblivion, but finally relief comes, and I'm temporarily free from all my stress and concern.

It's a good thing I have that chance to take a break because tomorrow I will discover a fatal error that will increase my stress level tenfold. In my rush for slumber, I've neglected a key task that will have me cursing my own name almost the very moment I wake up. In fact, the battle to make it to Swing Dance Club tomorrow is only just beginning.

Chapter 10

The next morning I awake to a hard smack to the head that sends me reeling back across the bed, arms flailing. I'm so groggy that it takes me a while to realize that my third roommate, Chris, is standing over me. That's never a good sign.

"You left your crap in the kitchen again."

I look down to see my laptop, which was what had woken me up. He probably dropped it on my head.

"Sorry, dude."

"Don't give me sorry. Just get it out of here."

For someone with no job and seemingly no plan in life, he can be awfully demanding. I sat up and hit the power button on my laptop, thinking I'd do a quick touch up on the paper now that I have fresh eyes. Chris leaves for wherever he spends 97% of the time. If I can even just fix a few typos, that will be a good start to the morning.

I look down at my laptop screen to see that it's still black. I must not have pushed the button hard enough. I hit it again, but it still does nothing. For a hot second I think Chris broke it somehow. Then I plug the charger in, and the little light turns on. It's out of battery. Wait, did I actually turn off my computer, or just put it in sleep mode? I dive under the covers again, already knowing the answer. I don't want to face it. I know I have to, but I really, really don't want to see it with my own eyes. When did I last save? How much do I have to do again? I need to know so I can plan out my strategy. I pull the covers over my head more tightly. Then I remember Charlotte's shaking voice last night and sit up. I'm in a world of pain, both physically from the lack of sleep and mentally from my monumental screw up. All of that can wait.

I turn my laptop on and pull up the word processor. My heart skips a beat. There is a recovery file. Suddenly I can breathe again. I click on it and immediately look down at the page count. Seven. Most of it is still here. I scan through it quickly. All the sections are there, but the part speaking to the general principles of Organic Chemistry are gone. It's a big hit, but a survivable one. I only have about fifteen minutes before I have to leave for class, but I'm going to spend as much of it as possible trying to redo what I lost. I throw on some new clothes and some deodorant, not even bothering to shower. I don't have time for it this morning.

Luckily, I remember some of what I wrote yesterday, so I'm able to recreate a decent chunk of it before I have to go. I push it to the point I'll have to literally sprint to get to class on time and then head out. I save the paper to my cloud storage out of sheer paranoia, grab my backpack and charger, and make a run for it.

I'm hoping to be able to keep working on the paper during class, but luck has completely abandoned me today. We have a pop quiz that takes half of class time and the rest of it is a review for the test that I can't zone out of because the professor hints very strongly at the material that will actually be on the test. Studying will be a nightmare if I check out.

My next class is a general literature class that's all the way across campus. Attendance in that one is part of the grade, so once again I can't skip. The professor for that one is a bit of a stickler and doesn't allow any device usage during class, but I'm so hammered from lack of sleep that it's actually kind of nice to take a forced break.

By the end of class it's nearly lunchtime, and I'm so famished it's hard to say whether hunger or tiredness is taking more out of me. It's obviously going to be more efficient to spend my time eating right now because then I'll be able to get more done with whatever amount of time I can scrounge together between my third and fourth classes today. But just as I'm trying to figure out which vending machine is closest, my phone rings. This time it isn't Charlotte. It's far worse than that. It's my father.

I pick up, because if I don't and he finds out I don't have a good excuse, it will cause more problems than missing another meal.

"What's up, Dad?"

"Why is the balance of the checking account so low?" he asks in his normal thick accent. He's from Bangladesh and immigrated here when he was seventeen. He's worked like a dog his whole life, so I guess it's to be expected that he holds tightly to his money as much as possible. Still, it does make life stressful.

"They already charged me tuition for next semester."

"Twelve thousand dollars? For one semester?" We've been over this several times before, but he still sounds half a step away from suing me for fraud. "The money in that account for school! Not for partying. If you spend it drinking, you will not be getting any more."

I could practically recite his lecture from memory.

"I won't, I promise."

"Good. And one more thing. Are you still trying to get into medical school?"

"Yes, Dad."

Every time he asks, it feels like he's hoping I'll have changed my mind.

"Don't forget. You don't make it in, you pay back the money I'm giving you."

"Yeah, I know, Dad."

"Good. Good work. I need to go now, goodbye."

He signs off abruptly, as is his custom. I knew exactly what he was going to say, but somehow hearing it again for the thousandth time makes me abandon my plans to buy an overpriced hot pocket. Instead I head to the engineering building, where, I happen to know, they hold a lecture series every Thursday at noon. I've never been all that into engineering, but have found myself there several times throughout the school year because they give out free pizza to attendees. If I was really aggressive about it, I could probably find some type of free food most days out of the week, but I usually don't have enough time for that with all my premed homework. Today I'm particularly desperate.

I can't work on the paper during the presentation as that would be rude, but hopefully I'll be able to be more productive if I'm not so hungry. The lecture is about building parts for satellites and space shuttles essentially out of origami with metal and other fancy materials. At any other time, I'd be at least mildly interested. Today I'm really struggling. The light is a bit dim, and the speaker's voice a bit monotonous. No one's looking at me. Surely no one will notice if I close my eyes for a second.

I'm sledgehammered awake for the second time today. This time it's slightly more gentle. One of the engineering professors is standing over me, shaking my shoulder.

"Sorry to wake you, but we have a class starting here in ten minutes."

I gaze blearily up at him for a few seconds before his words register. I'm too sleepy to even be properly embarrassed. It's only as I stand up and sling my backpack over my shoulder that I see the empty pizza boxes huddled on a table in the corner, and the full implications of what has just happened smacks me in the face. It may well be the saddest sight I've ever seen.

"Ah. S-sorry," I stammer and make a hasty retreat.

I sprint to class for the second time today. It's so miserable that it's honestly pretty hilarious. I don't know why that makes it better, but somehow it does.

I slide into my seat a couple of minutes late. Given the circumstances, that's actually not too bad, but I still feel a sting of shame when I lock eyes with the professor. Maybe because of that, I can't bring myself to work on the paper during his class. It doesn't help that it feels like my intestines are trying to strangle me from the inside for lack of food. With every faculty of body and mind screaming at me, very little of the lecture actually makes it into my brain. Still, I can't collapse yet.

I stagger to my feet the moment we're dismissed. It would probably be best for me to just go back home and sleep the day away at this point, because it's obviously not going to get any better. But I'm not about to let Charlotte down. I have class from four to five thirty that has an in-class assignment that I can't miss, and then I have to get to Lindsay's place by six, which is a good fifteen-minute walk away, meaning this is the last chance I'll have to work on it.

So I go back inside and set up my laptop again for the umpteenth time. Luckily, my next class is in this building too, so I can spend the whole time working. By this point, though, I'm so out of it that my progress is literally at a snail's pace. It takes me a good ten minutes just to find where I left off.

After just a couple of sentences, the urge to throw in the towel and curl up on the bench to take a nap suddenly rushes over me. I force myself to picture Charlotte totally falling apart on stage tonight without me there. I can't let that happen. Just another sentence. Just a few more words.

Why am I doing this to myself? Is showing up to a single club meeting really going to make such a big difference? Is she honestly going to take one look at me standing there, and suddenly that's going to solve everything? It's not like I have an anti-panic-attack wand up my sleeve. My hands fall to my sides. But then—*You make me feel...safe.* My mind hears her say the words a second time. Okay. One more line.

My eyes pop open again, and I immediately look at the clock to see how long I've been asleep. Whew, it's been just a few minutes. I type another sentence. Then another. The whole world is blending together in an awful, soupy mush. Should I take a break to check social media? No, stay focused. I can sleep when I'm done.

The next two hours limp by. With twenty minutes left until my next class, I finally finish section two for the second time. I set an alarm on my phone and allow myself a brief nap. I don't have to be exactly lucid, but I will need some amount of brain function for the meetup later. Frustratingly, now that I'm actually *trying* to sleep, it's awfully difficult to get there. *The more you think, the less sleep you'll get,* my brain says unhelpfully.

Brrring! Brring! I snap awake, not even aware that I'd drifted off. My sanity is slightly more intact, but not by much. It will have to do for now. I drag myself around the corner into the appropriate lecture hall. I still can't focus, but now it's more because I'm starting to worry about whether I've done enough for my group not to eviscerate me. The next hour has to be one of the longest in human history. Someone must have slipped and hit the button to play the lecture at one-fourth speed. It's quite a dry lecture in its own right, but at the moment I don't even think a live demonstration of dynamite could have caught my attention. I review the route to Lindsay's apartment in my mind. Where's Swing Dance Club again? In the student center, right?

At the end of class, I'm the first one out the door. I'm really not up to sprinting, but I try to walk relatively fast. I've got to wrap things up and head back here as quickly as possible. There's no way I'm making it on time, but fashionably late is still on the table.

I make it there fifteen minutes early, but no one else is there. I guess I can't blame them; I didn't really make it clear that I wanted to be as fast as possible today. There isn't really a place to set up my laptop here, so I just pace back and forth restlessly. I text Charlotte to let her know I'm still coming so she won't freak out that I'm not there yet. There's no response.

I'm about ready to tear my hair out when Lindsay drives up. She looks surprised to see me so early.

"I did a bunch of it last night," I explain. "I'm hoping I can get you guys started here and then leave early.

She shrugs.

"I'm fine with that, but I don't know about Raymond."

That makes both of us.

Lindsay unlocks the door and lets me in. Her apartment is a little smaller than mine, but only three people live here instead of four, so it isn't any more cramped, really. Aside from a bit more effort on the decoration front, it feels quite similar.

"Looks like you have some good roommates," I say noting the lack of dishes in the sink.

"Well, in some ways," she says, "They're good at cleaning up after themselves, but they're always watching loud movies late into the night." I wince appreciatively. I'm glad my own roommates don't do that. Just as I'm thinking that, there's a knock at the door. It's Raymond.

"Let's get this show on the road," he says, sliding into a chair.

"This should be pretty fast. I actually did most of it yesterday," I say pulling out my laptop.

"You—what?" says Lindsay. "I thought you said you just got started on it.

"Well I didn't do *all* of it..."

"You can't just write a group paper without our input," says Raymond. "I can't put my name on a project I didn't help with."

"I—" This wasn't the problem I had foreseen here. "You did contribute, though! I used a lot of the elements we talked about last time. Also, there's a lot of the third section I haven't done yet."

His expression doesn't change, telling me this isn't a good enough answer.

"Hey, why don't you look over what I have and see what needs to be changed? Just think of it as a rough draft."

Raymond wordlessly pulls the laptop toward him.

"You misspelled titration. E1 reactions are through a carbocation intermediate, not a carbocation substrate. You forgot to talk about the limitations of the studies you're citing," he says tonelessly.

I'm shriveling up inside. I glance over at Lindsay, hoping for some sympathy, but she just shrugs. Come on guys! I did a bunch of work for you. How is that something to be mad about? Also, I really need to be on my way. The clock is ticking.

Raymond makes a big show of editing the first section. I don't dare interrupt him, seeing how upset he is.

"You didn't talk about how elimination reactions compare to other types of reactions," he says finally. I wait to see if there's anything else, but he falls mercifully silent.

"Well, look. I have to get going right now, but at least this leaves you something to contribute, right?"

If looks could kill, the laser beams Raymond sends my way would have skewered me to the wall.

"Are you kidding me?"

"What?"

"Are you *SERIOUS*?"

I shrink beneath his gaze.

"Well, I was hoping that if I got enough done--"

"And you think that *Swing Dance Club* is important enough to risk our futures?" he interrupts. "You realize you're not the only one trying to get into graduate school, right?"

"He did do an awful lot--" says Lindsay.

"That's not the issue," Raymond cuts Lindsay off as well. "The issue is that we're supposed to do this as a *team*."

"I know it's kind of a dumb reason," says Lindsay, "but--"

"No," says Raymond, rising from his chair and bringing all of his six-foot-two frame to bear on me, "You are not leaving until this thing is done."

I'm dying inside. I feel myself bending under the weight of his pressure, like a steel beam beneath a bridge that's too big for it. It's not that I suddenly agree with him; I don't. It's more like his opinion is so massive that it's completely engulfing my own, making it all but impossible for me to even see it, let alone articulate it.

After all that effort, a wall has sprung up that I can't surmount. It's not even me that I'm angry for. It's that look of betrayal that's going to appear on Charlotte's face the moment she finds out I've let her down. I blink back bitter tears.

"All right," I tell him as my heart breaks in two. "Let's do this."

Chapter 11

I watch the time trickle by. The paper is slowly coming together, but it's certainly not going to be a short job. I try to push back the guilt with thoughts of all the people I'm going to help once I'm a doctor. It doesn't work. My heart is still trying to tear open my chest from the inside. *But surely her life isn't going to fall apart over a couple of musical numbers,* my mind tries to convince me. *She'll understand once I explain it to her, right?*

Lindsay looks over at me from the section she's proofreading. I nod back at her and scroll back through our list of sources. My father would be furious if he saw me letting a silly little club meeting get in the way of school. *Get your priorities straight, Levi. There's no way this is going to matter five years from now.*

Raymond points out another typo. I fix it, the avalanche of excuses in my head continuing to build. My group members are counting on me. It isn't fair to risk their grade over something so trivial. Charlotte will probably be just fine even without me. *I don't really have a choice here,* I think, closing my laptop with a snap. It's not like Charlotte hasn't done her fair share of flaking out on me lately. I pack my chemistry textbook and my notes into my backpack, closing it with a quick zip. It's not like her parents will magically stop pressuring her to quit singing just because I'm there. I load my laptop into my backpack and stand. Raymond looks up at me inquiringly.

Yes, the only reasonable answer here is to finish the paper and apologize profusely later. Life isn't always about getting what I want.

"Sorry, guys," I tell them. "I really have to go."

No, sometimes it's about doing what's right no matter what.

For the third time today, I turn and run, checking the time as I go. It's 6:25, which is bad, but not nearly as bad as it could have been. I'll still get there well before Charlotte sings.

I consider texting her to tell her I'm on my way, but I don't want to risk it while running, and every moment I spend slowing down is a moment more I'm letting her down. I can do this.

At 6:35 I stumble back to campus. Student center, student center, that's by the stadium, isn't it? I head over there. Swing dancing is a fairly noisy activity, so I should be able to find it fairly easily. At least that's what I think until I actually get inside. The entryway is completely empty, almost unnervingly so. I can't hear anything but the air whooshing in and out of my lungs. No matter, I'll just have to take it one hallway at a time. This building isn't that big.

I race to the end of the hallway and peer down the next one. It is also completely desolate. I flash down it, checking the rooms on either side as I go just to be sure. Nothing. At the end I turn right and keep going. Did they cancel the club meeting for some reason? After a couple more hallways of the same, I'm starting to get desperate. It finally occurs to my sleep-deprived mind that maybe I should just look up the location online. In all my frantic rushing yesterday I didn't even consider that. Search Engine. School Website. Search Bar. Scan through the results. Nothing. Really? Wait, what about searching for the generic club page?

There it is. It's in the Tanner Building. I take off running again without even bothering to check the time even though I urgently want to know it. Of course the Tanner building is most of the way back across campus. Now that I think about it, it makes sense that the club would meet there because it has actual ballrooms that the dance majors use for classes.

There are still enough people here and there to give me weird looks as I run past. I feel a bit embarrassed in spite of myself, but that doesn't stop me. Rounding the corner of the art museum, I slip on some loose gravel and go down hard. I bounce back up again with a stinging in my knee that I don't bother to check on. As I burst through the doors of the Tanner Building, I hear music drifting down the hall. It's a good sign. As long as I can get there by the end, that's all that matters now. I sprint towards the sound, lungs screaming at me to stop.

I burst into the ballroom the music is coming from right as it shuts off. Everyone immediately turns and stares at me, and I suddenly real;ize how this must look. A sweaty, exhausted, heaving wretch of a human desperately trying to make it to--Swing Dance Club? It's a blessing that I'm not very lucid right now because otherwise I would be dying inside. Swiftly I scour the room for Charlotte, but she's nowhere to be seen. Oh no. I check my phone for messages, but there are none.

"Levi!"

I whirl around, half expecting a miracle, only to come face to face with: Mara? My overtaxed brain simply cannot compute and abruptly shuts down.

"Hi, I'm here."

She laughs, but not in a mean way. The people standing around seem to see this interaction as at least a partial explanation of my strange appearance and go back to what they were doing, which now that I'm paying attention, seems to be packing up for the evening.

"You're in Swing Dance Club?" I hazard.

"I'm not really a diehard member. I just show up every once in a while."

"That's cool." I suddenly become acutely aware of the fact that I haven't showered today and somehow ended up going out in public wearing a T-shirt depicting a wolf eating a watermelon. The characteristic awkward silence begins to form like a malevolent fog, but to my surprise, Mara's the one who breaks it.

"You seemed to be—in a hurry."

"Yeah, uh, I was looking for someone. Do you know Charlotte who goes to this club?"

"Oh yeah, she left a couple of minutes ago."

Now I really am dying inside.

"Ugh. I really need to find her. Maybe I could try her apartment?"

"You look awful."

"Thanks, I try."

"You're bleeding, by the way."

I look down to see the knee of my jeans soaked with blood from my fall earlier.

"This day has been an ant-infested Twinkie."

There's suddenly a touch of softness in Mara's eyes.

"I think I've got a band-aid in my backpack."

I follow her over to her backpack leaning up against the wall. She pulls out a full-on first-aid kit complete with band-aids, syringes, burn cream, and antiseptic wipes. Her fingers leap to the last of these. She hands me one along with the band-aid.

"I guess it pays to be friends with a nursing student." Maybe it's just the tiredness numbing my brain, but I'm a lot less nervous talking to Mara than normal

"Yes, you should really take one with you wherever you go. Seriously, though, you look awful."

"I was up pretty late working on a paper and have been running myself ragged all day."

Literally.

"I guess it was pretty important to you to find Charlotte." she says, wiping my knee with antiseptic a bit harder than is strictly necessary. I mentally facepalm.

"So the thing is—"

"Are you hungry?"

"Yes!" I say with more enthusiasm than I intended. She chuckles a little again.

"Wanna grab something?"

I look down at what I'm wearing. Mara follows my gaze.

"It's chill. It's not like we're going to a Michelin star restaurant or something."

My heart catches up with my brain and begins to pound.

"Sure, if you don't mind me sweating like a racehorse."

"Swing dancing is pretty active too, you know."

"That's true. Okay, then."

She grabs my hand and hoists me to my feet. She does it so casually that I don't even realize until we are most of the way out of the ballroom that she just voluntarily touched me. My heart pounds a little harder.

By sheer luck we end up right next to the table where I sat with Charlotte yesterday. Was it really only yesterday? Mara opts for a cheeseburger today, while I get a pan pizza. It's going to be a while before I buy a gyro again after what happened last time. Once again the sheer tiredness seems almost helpful because I'm not nearly as nervous as I feel like I should be. In fact, because of the length of time I've been anticipating asking her out, it feels a bit surreal. Not that Mara necessarily sees this as a date, but it's close enough that I don't care.

You should text Charlotte and let her know why you didn't make it, my brain tells me. But then I'd have to think about how badly I failed her. I know I'm going to have to cross that bridge at some point, but I really don't want to.

I bite into my pan pizza, and suddenly all of this flies out the window. I am *so hungry*.

"This was a good idea," I pronounce. "I haven't eaten anything since yesterday."

"Since yesterday? Holy cow! How are you still upright?"

"Well the sight of you certainly helps," I say without thinking. Mara blushes, and I realize that maybe it's not such a bad thing to have less of a filter today. Forget alcohol, extreme tiredness is my liquid courage.

"How about you, busy day?" I ask.

"Pretty busy. I have a couple of tests coming up, but nothing out of the ordinary."

"I bet the nursing program is usually pretty intense."

She shrugs.

"It's not too bad. There are definitely hard parts, for sure. Drawing blood isn't really my thing."

"I bet it really sucks the life out of you."

Mara laughs, a clear, melodic sound that makes me want to hear it again as soon as possible.

"What got you into nursing?"

Mara's smile vanishes and I freak out, thinking I've said the wrong thing, but she doesn't brush off the question.

"A long time ago someone important to me had a medical emergency while I was with them, and I totally dropped the ball. I don't want to feel like that ever again."

People try to be nice because they don't want to feel guilty, says the little Micah in the back of my head. I tell him to take a hike.

"Dropping the ball is the worst."

As soon as the words are out of my mouth, I realize I probably just came across as extremely callous. My brain flips into damage control mode, but it just isn't working fast enough. To my surprise, instead of being offended, Mara just nods. Then I realize my voice just now was dripping with self-criticism.

"I actually think that's an impressive reason," I continue. "It would be easy to be so afraid of messing up again that it makes you run the opposite direction."

She looks genuinely touched. To my shock, she reaches across the table and very deliberately puts her hand on top of mine.

"You're a really sweet guy, Levi."

My brain utterly short circuits.

"As sweet as Jello," it spazzes. For some reason, this makes Mara burst out laughing again. I rest my head on my arm as it starts pounding once more.

"I'm sorry, Mara. I'm so tired I can't think straight. I think we'll have to continue this some other time."

"I'd like that."

I takes me another second to realize that after weeks of agonizing and overthinking, I just asked Mara out literally by accident. Does it still count as an accident if it was what I wanted to do anyway? She pats my head fondly and heads out.

"See you around," she says. I take a second bite of pizza, but by now my need for sleep is stronger than my need for food, so I pack the rest up and make for my apartment. I cannot wait to fall into my warm, lumpy-but-familiar bed and leave this day behind. Good riddance.

Aren't I forgetting something?

I look and my phone, and my heart sinks. I have several missed calls and a couple of texts from Charlotte. The last one says:

Do you hate me?

It's taking some focus just to put one foot in front of the other, so it's a bit of a miracle that my thumb finds the coordination to hit the Call button. Of course, there's no way she's going to answer. She's going to tell me she didn't want to call me after all, just like she did yesterday.

"Hello?"

It takes me far too long to register that it is indeed a human voice coming from my phone, and that since I've just dialed Charlotte's number, it's probably her.

"Charlotte! I'm so sorry." I get out. "I tried *so hard* to be there. I didn't think--"

"Where are you?"

"I'm just leaving the food court. I think it's about--" I don't even know how I plan on finishing that sentence. The world swoons violently and I have to break off whatever it was to catch my balance.

"I'm sorry, Charlotte. I'm so sorry." My brain can't come up with the words to explain myself, so I'm just rambling on like a broken record, hoping the emotion of it gets the right idea across somehow. The world rocks again, and I have to lean against a nearby trashcan for support. A small part of me recognizes that something is horribly wrong with me, but it's far too tiny to do more than watch in growing horror as I stumble in the general direction of home.

"Levi!"

A voice is coming from somewhere, but I can't tell if it's from my phone or real life. I feel like I'm going to be violently ill. The combination of exhaustion, hunger, physical exertion, and stress has finally ground me to a halt. Luckily, there's a bench nearby. I sprawl headlong across it, not caring who's watching. The world is spinning like a whirlwind.

Someone's there, but I can't tell who. Hopefully it's someone who won't judge me.

This bench is really hard I think, right before I pass out.

Chapter 12

The whole world is still. I blink my eyes slowly, savoring the brief amnesia that rules the world between sleep and wakefulness. For this one golden moment I have no memory of where I am or how I got here. I just exist. It's beautiful. My next awareness is that someone is gently stroking my hair. I'm too sleepy to be bothered by that, but it does make me curious enough to open my eyes. The first thing I see is purple, the purple of Charlotte's gaze brushing softly against my own. She notices my eyes open but doesn't pull away in embarrassment the way I would have expected. Then I realize that my head is in her lap. That's almost enough for me to jerk away violently, but fortunately I'm out of it enough to delay that course of action until the rest of my brain can come up with a more diplomatic exit.

I try to sit up, but my insides churn dramatically. I'm forced to wait a few seconds for my body to get used to being awake again.

"I'm sorry," I tell Charlotte for the hundredth time. "I don't hate you, I promise. I was trying to get this paper done--"

She strokes my hair again, and the thought dies before I can get the words out. It isn't exactly unpleasant; it's just that *we're in freaking public.* I glance around surreptitiously, only to realize that it's quite dark out and no one's around. That makes Charlotte's behavior a little less strange, but I'm still awfully confused.

I finally regain enough internal stability to sit up. I get ready for Charlotte to playfully rake me over the coals as she does, but it never comes. She just sits there.

"Are you okay?" I ask.

"No," she says calmly.

"At least you're being honest about it now."

She nods with a stoicism that I can't interpret. A tear slides over her cheek.

"How did it go?" I ask.

"They gave my spot to someone else."

"What? Why? Wasn't it reserved for you?"

She shrugs.

"One of them was friends with the club president, I guess."

"They can't just do that!"

"Well they just did."

"And to top it all off, I stood you up. I really stepped in it this time."

She stares off into the distance.

"It's okay."

Why is she being like this?

"Charlotte, what is going on?"

"I'm not going to bother you anymore, Levi."

Something inside me breaks as she says that. I try to find the words that will turn the situation around, but nothing comes. There's an emptiness in her eyes that terrifies me.

"It was nice of you to try to look out for me, but I don't want to drag you down with me," she says quietly.

"That isn't the point," I say. "I just don't want you to have to deal with all this by yourself. You aren't dragging me down."

She gets to her feet and responds as if she hasn't heard me.

"I have a way of crushing everything I touch."
Another tear slides out. "I really, *really* don't want to
crush you."

I want to say something, anything to prove her
wrong. But how do you get someone to let go of what
they truly believe, even if it's awful?

Before I can conjure up a response, she ruffles my
hair tenderly in the exact spot Mara did and starts to
walk away.

"Wait!"

As she turns to look back at me, I see something
heartbreaking in her violet eyes. The doors to her heart,
which have miraculously been opening up a little at a
time since the flat tire in the rain, have slammed shut
again. Her trickle of tears swells into a torrent. I stand up
and take a couple of slow, dizzy steps toward her.

"Charlotte, please--"

"I don't want to be a burden to you."

I'm not in a position to run any foot races, so I can
only watch desperately as she walks away, allowing the
dark of the night to swallow her bit by bit.

"Charlotte--"

"Goodbye, Levi," she calls out without turning
around.

And just like that, she's gone.

Now the tears come for me as well. It's so *stupid*.
Thanks to my momentary loss of resolve earlier, I've
somehow managed to break Charlotte's trust *and* make
her feel like it's all her fault. If only I hadn't hesitated. If
only I hadn't let Mara's attention and Raymond's opinion
of me matter more than Charlotte's mental stability.
Then everything would be different. Now she's cut off
from me in a way that no simple text or phone call, no
matter how carefully worded, is going to be able to fix.
Making this right is going to take a miracle.

So I guess I'd better set about making one happen, then. I'm certainly not going to sit back and let her suffer for my mistakes. I still don't know how to help her with the panic attacks and money issues, but I'm going to figure it out. I *will* find a way to restore her trust and clear the way for her to become the singer she's trying to be, I promise myself.

No matter what it takes.

Chapter 13

I make it back to my apartment more worn down than a wooden chair under a belt sander. Micah tries to engage me in a conversation, but I brush him off and collapse onto my bed, not bothering to change out of my clothes for the second night in a row. When I wake up, the shattered pieces of the world have clicked back into place.

There's a bit of a scramble to finish a couple of assignments that I didn't do yesterday. For the most part, though, everything is much calmer. I don't try to contact Charlotte. Hounding her right now isn't going to accomplish anything. I do, however, check my phone throughout the day on the off chance that she's changed her mind and wants to talk to me anyway.

As morning turns to afternoon, the mental fog lifts a little. I start thinking about trying to talk to Mara again. I can't help but get a bitter taste in my mouth when I think about it, though, because my almost-date with her was the reason I missed Charlotte's call. Guilt devours my thoughts like a black hole feasting on passing light, leaving nothing but darkness. With effort, I pull myself out of it. Wallowing in mistakes isn't going to help anyone.

The afternoon glides by. As I finish the last class of the day and head for home, it occurs to me that Micah is probably there. For some reason that thought doesn't fill me with as much dread as it has recently. I've been avoiding him ever since he crashed my date with

Charlotte, but I can't just live on campus until he moves out. It's better to bite the bullet and face everything he's been saving up for me so I can actually relax again. Who knows? Maybe he'll actually go easy on me this time.

* * *

"Look what the cat dragged in," Micah says the second I walk through the door. There's a particularly irritating smirk on his face, and I know instantly that all my hopes were in vain and that I'm done for.

"Have you been running away from me?" he says slowly, savoring every word, "Or have you been running away from yourself?"

"I don't know why you're surprised I don't enjoy being torn to shreds over every little thing."

There's more he could say here, but the fact that he doesn't tells me that he's got something particularly juicy in store for me today.

"You sure went to a lot of effort to hide your girlfriend from me," he says with enough pleasure to make my skin crawl.

"She isn't my girlfriend," I say and then immediately realize that I've already fallen right into his trap.

"I don't know why you're bothering to lie to yourself. You looked awfully...involved."

"Not every interaction with a woman has to be about attraction."

"So you aren't attracted to her?"

I can't even look at him. Living at the library is starting to look better and better.

"So she's really not your girlfriend yet? Is she going to be?"

"No."

"Why not? It looked like she was into you."

"It's complicated."

"So you're repressing. That isn't healthy."

Even though I knew something like this was coming, I start to feel my blood beginning to boil in spite of myself.

"How would you know? You've never even had a girlfriend!"

"Ooh, I hit a nerve."

I almost say something I'd regret but manage to hold myself in check by the skin of my teeth. I want to retreat to the safety of my room, but if I do that, Micah's just going to accuse me of running away again. So I take a deep breath.

"I don't know why you're so obsessed with my dating choices."

"The only thing I'm obsessed with is not letting people lie to themselves."

"Is lying to yourself such a bad thing?"

To my surprise, Micah takes a moment to respond.

"It is if you want to make the most of yourself."

"What does that even mean?"

"Nietzsche said that greatness is wanting nothing to be different than it is. Not just enduring it, but fully embracing it without any self-deception."

"And who says I have to care about being great?"

Micah pauses again.

"All living things have a drive to expand their dominance over the world around them—a will to power. It's part of who you are."

"Ah. So that's why you're always trying to beat me in arguments. You're trying to dominate me intellectually."

"Nietzsche said that you have to surrender almost everything in order to wrestle for truth."

"Who's living your life? You? Or Nietzsche?"

Micah gives me a look I've never seen before. Wait a minute. Did I actually land a hit? He sits down at the table, and for a split second I let myself think I've won.

"At least I don't spend my time trying to pretend like my feelings don't exist. At least I don't run around trying to force silver linings onto everything because I can't tolerate the world being anything less than sunshine and rainbows. At least I have the courage to face the grim realities of life. At least I don't try to twist my life into something contorted and unnatural just because society tells me it has to be that way."

"What am I doing that's contorted and unnatural?"

The irritating smile that had momentarily vanished from his face returns again.

"You think I didn't notice you staying up until the crack of dawn doing homework yesterday? And all that work for a lie. You don't actually want to be a doctor. You just have no idea what to do with your life and feel like the story you've told your father *has* to be true because you've told it so many times. *That's* the risk of living a lie. Being trapped in a life you hate because you've built your expectations up so high that they've slowly become your own prison."

With that, he disappears back into his room, leaving me to deal with the emotional aftermath. He's not wrong. It's been a long time since I was actually excited about medical school. I've been telling myself and everyone around me that it was the dream for so long now that I didn't even notice when it stopped being true. Slowly over time its heavenly aura faded, so subtly that I didn't even notice it leaving. Now it's more of what I expect myself to want rather than something that actually sounds appetizing. The terrifying thing is that I'm in too deep to back out now.

I stare down at a tiny diorama of a building Micah made for his art history class. Fittingly, it's an ancient Geek temple. *Does that man ever think about anything other than philosophy?* I wonder.

Although my conversation with Micah went far worse than I had hoped, at the very least my plan worked in that I've gotten it over with and can now breathe freely again. He still pops in and out, but he's fulfilled his philosophical wrangling quota for the moment. I shouldn't have to worry about him for a while. It's nice to have another human being around to stave off the silence. For some reason, it's been especially deafening lately. So back to the mindless minutia it is, at least until Thursday, when I'll make another attempt to talk to Charlotte at Swing Dance Club. My hope is that after a few days of space, she'll be willing to at least give me the time of day again.

The next two days are quite busy, which is a good thing because having time to think has not been my friend lately. It seems like everywhere I look, I see that telltale swish of blonde hair, those purple eyes. I can't help but wonder what it was that caused Charlotte to start having panic attacks in the first place. From what Mason said, it seems unlikely that they appeared out of nowhere. She either blames herself for whatever it was that happened or for how much she's struggled since then, and now she honestly believes she has to keep other people at arm's length for their own good. What a heartbreaking way to see the world.

And yet, despite everything she's been through, she's fighting tooth and nail for the right to keep singing. I've put a lot of effort into landing a spot in medical school, but this feels different somehow. It's partially because, unlike me, she actually *wants* to be a singer. I don't quite understand what it means to love something so much that you'd be willing to risk a mental meltdown in front of hundreds of people for the chance to keep doing it. I want to, though. At this, my inner Micah chimes in again.

Repressing! Repressing! I swiftly shoo him away. What I'm trying to do here honestly isn't being driven by attraction. In fact, I sense that if I were to allow myself to slip into that mindset, something important would be lost here. That doesn't mean I don't admire Charlotte, though. I do. A lot.

I fully expect the typical college-style drudgery to continue for the rest of the week, but I'm in for a huge shock. On the third day of my hiatus, something happens that upends the chicken coop. In fact, although I don't realize it at the moment, what happens on that day is a turning point that will end up sending my whole life careening sideways. It all starts with a knock on the door.

Chapter 14

I'm sitting on the couch in the middle of a particularly thorny calculus assignment when I hear the pounding. At first it doesn't register that it's coming from the door. Our apartment is not exactly the social nexus of campus. In fact, aside from the occasional family member, I can't remember ever having visitors. So it isn't until I hear the rapping a second time that it dawns on me what's happening. At first the irrational part of my brain thinks it could be Charlotte wanting to patch things up until I remember that she has no idea where I live. I suppose it could be someone for Micah or Chris. I chuckle at the very thought as I reach for the knob.

Standing in the doorway is someone I've never seen before. He's about a head shorter than I am and mildly stocky with a slight color to his skin. There's a very serious expression on his face, but part of that may be the huge pair of sunglasses he's sporting.

"Can I help you?"

He doesn't say anything at first, but tries to peek past me through the doorway. Odd. I reflexively step forward and pull the door closer to me to make it harder on him, although I've no idea why he would want to inspect the empty interior of my apartment in the first place.

"Can I help you?" I repeat a little more forcefully.

A giant smile breaks across his face.

"Ah, sorry. I am Ajay," he says. "I moved in recently," he gestures vaguely at the apartment across from Mara's. "I'm trying to meet everybody."

"Oh! Okay." I relax a little. "Are you a student?"

"Yes. This is my first semester."

"Got it. So why are you moving in the middle of the term?"

"There was a—situation with one of my roommates that I had to get away from. Luckily, I was able to find a contract for sale here. I almost thought I was going to have to sleep on a park bench."

He gives a forced chuckle, which quickly fades to awkward silence. Not that I'm one to judge when it comes to social ineptness. If anything, it makes me feel more comfortable.

"Well, cool. People don't really talk to each other here, so I'm glad someone friendly moved in."

"Yeah, yeah. We should go out for drinks sometime."

"I don't drink. Sorry, man."

"Go out on the town, then."

"Sure. Not this week, though. Homework is kicking my butt right now."

"For sure! Give me your number, and I'll hit you up!"

I read it off to him, and he immediately types it into his phone.

"What's your major?" I ask.

He pauses a little too long.

"Photography," he says unconvincingly. I tilt my head a little.

"Isn't that a major you have to apply for? How did you get into it during your first semester?"

"I'm...a transfer student."

Now Ajay is giving off awfully weird vibes. I'm not sure whether to shut the door as quickly as possible or to try to get at whatever he's up to.

"Do you have a girlfriend?" He asks suddenly.

"No."

He looks disappointed for some reason.

"You must go on a lot of dates."

"Uh, I wouldn't say a lot..." This is getting weirder by the second.

"You should! You'd be a big hit with the ladies. We should double sometimes."

"Sure," I say a second time, but with far less enthusiasm. I'm starting to really regret giving him my number. I hope he doesn't try anything weird with Mara, being next door neighbors and all.

"Well, see you around," I say and start to close the door.

"Wait!"

I pause *very* grudgingly.

"Do you know anyone with purple eyes?"

"What?" My grip on the door slackens. I have an extremely bad feeling about this. "Purple eyes? Like contacts?"

I know exactly how to play it off because I've heard the reactions so many times.

"No, not contacts. Here, let me show you." He pulls out his phone again and taps the screen a few times.

"Here." He hands it over.

I look down at it to see—Charlotte. It's a much younger version of her, but it's pretty unmistakable. Her hair's much shorter, and she has a tattoo on her upper arm. That surprises me, although now that I think of it, I've never seen her wear tank tops or shirts with especially short sleeves. In the picture she looks to be about seventeen and has a particularly grouchy look on her face. There's something weird about the photo, though. I can tell it wasn't taken with this phone. It looks more like a picture that's been scraped from the internet. *Some photography major.*

"Why are you looking for her?" I ask, trying to come off as much less concerned than I actually am.

"We go way back. I heard that she goes to this school, but I haven't seen her in a long time."

I heard that she goes to this *school.* Someone who was actually a student here would say *our* school, right? Just as it dawns on me that I should try to get some identifying information from him, he says:

"Well, let me know if you see her," and heads back the way he came.

I watch him go. He rounds the corner of the apartment across from Mara's, but the door is out of sight, so I can't see whether he goes in or not. Drat. If I knew more about him, I could maybe get the school to check into whether he actually goes here, but knowing just a first name is not enough to go off of. Maybe Mara knows something. I glance back at my homework waiting for me forlornly on the couch. I was just on the verge of catching up for the week, but it looks like I'm about to have another late night. I head for Mara's apartment. Ajay's nowhere in sight when I get there, but that doesn't mean anything because he could be anywhere by now.

Mara isn't home, but her roommate tells me she's doing clinicals on campus. I ask her for her number and give her a quick call. The irony that *this* is the way I finally get her number does not escape me. She answers almost immediately.

"Hello?"

"It's Levi."

"Oh hey!" Her voice brightens.

"Do you have a second?"

"Uh, not right now, but if you give me about ten minutes, I'll be free. Just come up to the nursing department.

I was just going to talk to her over the phone, but I'm not about to turn down a chance to see her in person. "Got it. See you."

"See you."

I head out immediately, pausing just long enough to pull on a hoodie because it's been getting chillier in the evenings lately. Not having a car really sucks sometimes.

A few minutes later I'm standing in front of the elevator leading to the nursing department for the second time. For some reason, I don't feel nervous about meeting Mara like I would for a date. It's probably because there are a lot of other things on my mind right now. She's waiting for me just off the elevator landing as I arrive at the nursing department. Her hair looks spectacular despite obviously being trapped in a scrub cap all day. I almost tell her that, but that's not really why I'm here.

"Can we go somewhere private?"

A flood of emotions rush across her face, and I realize what I've just implied.

"No, it's not that! I just need your help with something."

Mara looks...relieved? Disappointed? It's hard to say.

"Yeah, we can talk in the office."

She leads me over to it and unlocks the door. It's a bit dim, even when she turns the light on, and the fact that there are no outside windows makes it feel a bit dismal. From the looks of it, the space seems to be shared by several nursing students. Maybe it's a place for TA's to grade papers? It's a little cluttered, but not more than to be expected. She closes the door behind her.

"What's up?"

For a brief moment, the fact that I'm alone with her paralyzes my thoughts with its sweet nectar, but I take a deep breath and refocus on the task at hand.

"You know the guy who moved into the apartment right next to yours?"

She looks confused.

"You mean in the next apartment complex over?"

"No, the one with a door right across from yours."

"You said it was a guy?"

I nod, unsure what that has to do with anything.

"The apartment across from mine is all girls."

My heart starts pounding again, but for a completely different reason from a second ago.

"He was looking for Charlotte."

Mara looks concerned, but not nearly as much as she should be.

"Maybe he's a classmate?"

"Then he would have just said so. I can't think of a good reason for him to lie."

"An ex-boyfriend?"

"That would only make me more worried. He was so *creepy*."

Mara doesn't seem to be getting it.

"Why is it that whenever I talk to you, it's always something related to Charlotte?"

There's a bit of an edge to her voice.

"Seriously? There's some stalker trying to find her for who knows what and that's what you're thinking about?"

"It's a little strange, I guess, but it doesn't really seem like our concern. He obviously has no idea where she is, so she should be fine, right? It's not like he was threatening her."

That's true, I guess, but my gut tells me that there's something more to it than that.

"How did he know that I knew her, though? That seems pretty sus to me. And he had a *picture* of her."

"Yeah, I guess that is a bit creepy. What is there to even do about it, though?"

"At the very least we can warn her," I say pulling out my phone and texting her. "I don't have any way to find him, so I guess the only other thing we can do is keep an eye out. You'll let me know if you see anyone suspicious hanging around, right?"

"Yeah." She seems a little reluctant still. She's not wrong that this is not really any of our concern, but it's still weird to me that she's dragging her feet so much about something that could very well be dangerous. Something's off.

"Hey, are you okay?" I think to ask. She looks surprised at the question.

"I'm...hanging in there," she says quietly.

"Ah, that explains it. I was wondering why you were being like this."

"What do you mean, 'being like this'?" She says with a certain intensity.

"Never mind. Don't worry about it."

She catches me by the shoulder.

"What do you mean, 'being like this'?"

I sigh, cursing my loose tongue.

"You're making light of something that might turn out to be pretty serious. That doesn't seem like you."

She goes quiet for a moment.

"How well do you know Charlotte?" she asks finally.

"What is that supposed to mean?"

"Let's put it this way: When you have as many skeletons in the closet as she does, it's no surprise if one or two of them crops up for air."

How would *Mara* know Charlotte's dirty laundry? I guess they do both go to Swing Dance Club, but still--

"If she has a dark past, isn't that all the more reason to be careful here? That only makes it more likely that she's at risk of getting hurt."

"All I'm saying," says Mara with a bitterness I've never heard from her before, "is that sometimes when somebody makes their bed, it's best to let them lie in it."

It's then that it fully dawns on me that I've only scratched the surface of what's going on between the two of them.

"I'll keep an eye out for the stalker, Levi," says Mara with resignation but also sincerity. "Don't worry about it."

"Thanks." I say. "That's all I'm asking for."

I head back toward home, since there doesn't seem to be anything more I can do at this point and my homework isn't going to do itself. As long as Charlotte knows what to look out for, it should be fine. Speaking of which, I wonder if she's responded yet. I pull out my phone to check. There is a notification, but it looks odd for some reason. I tap it. It's not a text message.

Free MSG: Unable to send message—message blocking active.

What?

I stop walking. I have to read the message three times until I understand what it means. *She blocked me? Why?* There's a stinging sensation in my chest, and I can't help but feel like she's sliding further and further out of reach. And of all the awful timing! It's unlikely that she's in any immediate danger, but I'd still better try to find her, just to be safe. The irony of me being so concerned about someone stalking Charlotte after having worked so hard to try to find her myself does not escape me. *Maybe Mara is right and I'm overthinking this.* But Ajay really was acting awfully strangely. Too much caution here is probably better than too little.

Even though it's much earlier in the day than my last visit, Charlotte's apartment is still incredibly dark. I don't know where else she would be, though, and I have no other way of getting in contact with her, so I knock.

Please be here, Charlotte. I don't want to have to hunt you down again. Finally the doorknob turns. *Yes!*

It's not Charlotte. Instead a pair of blue eyes peer back at me to complement dark black hair that comes down to the girl's ears. The curtains behind her are drawn, and even the sliver of the interior I can see seems awfully…dismal. I regain my composure.

"Is Charlotte here?"

"No."

The answer is so short and curt that I'm really not sure what to say to it.

"Do you know when she will be?"

"No."

I pull my jacket more tightly against my body, as if that's going to warm up the chilly vibes I'm getting from her.

"Can you tell her that Levi stopped by?"

"Sure," she says in a way that gives me absolutely no confidence that it's actually going to happen.

"All right, then," I say awkwardly. She closes the door sharply without so much as a goodbye. I stand there a moment more, trying to figure out where to go from here. My own feelings about it aside, this is not a good time for Charlotte to drop off the face of the earth. I grit my teeth and think again longingly of my homework sitting waiting for me at home. This is going to be a long night.

Chapter 15

I'm out of breath by the time I reach the campus police. I didn't quite run here, but I'd really rather not try to survive another day on three hours of sleep tomorrow, so I'm still trying to move relatively quickly. As soon as I see the female officer in uniform behind the desk with an expression sharp enough to dice cold steel, the nerves kick in. I hope that going to the police doesn't turn this into a bigger deal than it needs to be. I don't have a good way of contacting Charlotte right now, though, and they should at least be able to give her a heads up and keep a lookout for Ajay.

I pace back and forth in front of the entrance, heart pounding. I don't know how to explain this in a way that's going to make sense. I wonder if it might not be better just to wait until Swing Dance Club and talk to her then. But there's no guarantee that she's going to be there, especially if she's still trying to avoid me. I'm not about to let my insecurities pressure me into leaving her safety up to chance, so I tell my anxiety to take a hike and walk in the door.

"Yes?" says the officer with only slightly less ice layering her voice than Charlotte's roommate.

"I think there's someone stalking my friend," I get out. Somehow the words just feel *wrong,* like a professor is going to pop out from behind the desk and dock me points for making my explanation too clunky.

"Go on."

He—uh was wandering around my apartment asking weird questions. He told these bizarre lies about being a student and said he was looking for her."

"How do you know he was lying?"

"He, uh, just seemed like he was," I reply, my brain completely falling out of my head. How did I know that again? Oh yeah! The photography thing.

"He said it was his first semester in the photography program, but photography is a program you have to apply for."

"Maybe he's a transfer student."

"That—is what he said."

The officer sighs like I've just made her day ten times more exhausting.

"I'll make a note of it."

"He was acting *quite* strange. Is there any way you can warn her, just in case?"

The officer narrows her gaze.

"You haven't told her?"

"I couldn't get a hold of her."

"Mmhmm." The officer sighs again.

"All right. We'll reach out to her."

I let out a breath. That's something, right? Her roommate's got a popsicle's chance in the Gobi Desert of passing my message along, but this is a professional, right? Surely she will do it, if only for the sake of doing her job?

I leave the building even more uncertain than before I entered it. I don't think I did the best job explaining just how sketchy Ajay was, but here we are. What am I going to do, set up security cameras? I'm tempted by that idea more than I'd care to admit. No, as loath as I am to acknowledge it, there really isn't anything else to be done here. With a defeated sigh, I head for home, trying to put it out of my mind as much as possible. If I let this bother me much, I'm going to have a hard time focusing on homework, and that's not going to do anyone any good.

I'm so absorbed in my own thoughts I almost don't notice the person creeping through the parking lot next to me. Fortunately, there's something odd enough about their movements to grab my attention. I look over and suddenly there he is: Ajay, crouching down by a parked car, obviously trying to be inconspicuous by doing the exact things that are making him as conspicuous as possible. We're by another apartment complex, but not one that has any connection to myself or Charlotte that I'm aware of.

I almost freeze in my tracks, but realize in the nick of time that stopping suddenly is only going to catch his attention the way his slow creeping through the parking lot caught mine. So instead, I round the back of the apartment building, careful to maintain my same speed and gait. My mind is spinning. Do I call the police again? But I don't really have anything more concrete on him than I did a few minutes ago. I should watch him for a little bit and see if he does anything criminal.

With this in mind, I walk the length of the building and round the corner yet again, approaching the parking lot from the far side. As I get to the edge of the parking lot, I slow down. I'm in shadow now, and Ajay's line of sight should be obscured somewhat by the dumpster in front of me. I crouch down behind it and slither up closer so that I can peer through the gap between the dumpster and the wall. Now, what is Mr. Shady up to?

It takes me a moment to spot him because he's crouched down far enough that I can't see him over the tops of the vehicles. Then I catch a glimpse of him darting from one line of cars to another. When I first saw him, my assumption was that he was going to talk to some of the residents to try to find someone who knows Charlotte. That's definitely not what's he's doing, though. As I watch more closely, he seems to be much more interested the cars themselves.

Is he going to steal one? my inner crime thriller enthusiast suggests immediately. But almost instantly I can see that isn't the case at all. He's moving from car to car, peering inside, and then quickly moving on to the next one. Trying to steal something out of one of them, maybe? But no, I don't hear any windows breaking, and he's moving way too fast to be able to see much of the dark interiors. I move a little closer, counting on how focused he is on the task at hand to make him less aware of my presence.

What is he looking for? After watching for another minute, I notice something odd. He's looking *just through the windshields*, not any of the side windows. Also, he's not actually stopping to look at every single car. Are there any patterns? Is he looking for a particular make and model, maybe? No, he's stopping a little too frequently for that. Suddenly it clicks. He's only looking at gray cars. I watch for a while longer to confirm my hypothesis. Yes, a variety of makes and models, but all gray. But then...what does that have to do with the windshields?

I crawl a little farther forward. I'm more exposed now than I'd like to be, but I feel like I'm on the verge of figuring this whole thing out. Surely he won't look over here in the next thirty seconds, right? He's moving a little closer to me, and that also helps. I try my best to track his eyes. Windshield. Windshield. Windshield. There's a sort of pattern to it, as though he's looking at the same spot every time. I take another half step forward, and my jacket catches on the lid of the dumpster beside me. Spooked, I jerk backward, fighting to free myself. The lid hits the side of the dumpster, sending a sharp, clear clanging sound to all corners of the parking lot.

If I were a swearing man, I would undoubtedly let one slip right now. Adrenaline pumping, I spin and make a run for it, hoping that I was fast enough that he didn't see me. Then comes the thudding of footsteps from the parking lot. Oh no! I have a brief vision of the garbage man finding my murdered corpse on the sidewalk tomorrow morning during his morning rounds. I make it around the corner and sprint down the sidewalk toward the main street, trying to get to a semi-populated area as quickly as possible. At the corner I turn left back around toward the parking lot, thinking that he won't expect me to go back the way I came. If I can just outspeed him...

I hit the jets. My sneakers slip dangerously on a bit of loose gravel on the sidewalk, but I manage to keep my balance. I glance down to better watch my step.

Wham!

He's got you. You're done for! My mind screams helpfully. I go down hard, only then realizing that the impact had come from the front, not the back. What did I run into? I scramble to my feet, getting ready to fight for my life. There's a person in front of me. Did I hit a random pedestrian?

No. It's Ajay. He doesn't seem to be trying to attack me, though. He fights his way to his feet as well, only to succumb to the same loose gravel that nearly downed me and fall again.

Suddenly the fear leaves. Why does *he* seem so frightened of *me*?

"What are you doing?" I ask finally.

Ajay makes it to his feet and takes a step as if to start running again, but then gives it up. *He was trying to escape,* I realize. *He wasn't trying to chase me. The footsteps I heard were him running the other way! And now he knows that I've recognized him, there isn't a reason to run anymore.*

Ajay tries and fails to come up with a suitable explanation, ending up sort of flapping his lips awkwardly without any sound coming out.

"You aren't very good at this, are you?" I observe.

"Don't push this so far that she ends up getting hurt," he says finally.

"Don't you dare touch her," I snap back. "I'm not afraid of your threats."

"I'm not going to back down," he says with an intensity that sends chills down my spine. It doesn't seem like he's going to attack me though, so I may as well try getting more information out of him.

"What's your last name?"

"As if you don't know."

An odd response.

"Why are you pretending to be a college student?"

"What's it to you?"

"So you admit that you aren't."

He gives me the smoldering sort of look I probably give Micah on a daily basis.

"Are you her ex?" I pry further.

"I don't have to tell you anything."

It looks like I've gotten as much as I'm going to from him.

"Look, if you don't want me to get the police involved, you'd better leave Charlotte alone," I tell him as forcefully as I can.

"The police?" His eyes widen in fear. "Who are you?"

"Someone who's not going to let you get to her."

At that he turns and runs. I think about trying to chase him down, but I'm not really sure what I'd do if I caught him. Drag him to the dollar store and lock him up with a pair of toy handcuffs? He turns the corner and runs out of sight.

After some internal debate, I decide against going back to the campus police. For one thing, I'd almost certainly mangle my explanation again. For another, I still don't have enough information for them to track him down. I'd better tell Charlotte as soon as I see her again, though. If he's willing to threaten anyone close to her, she really needs to know what's happening. What exactly did you get up to before college, Charlotte?

As I head for home for what seems like the millionth time today, a sobering thought occurs to me. What if Ajay is the reason for Charlotte's panic attacks? If he is her ex, that would make sense. Especially given that the last one came about because of an angry boyfriend. I feel another spike of anger at the thought. That gives me yet another reason to make sure he can't find her. She's going to have a difficult enough time healing without demons reemerging from the shadows and ripping open old scars. The more I learn about Charlotte's past, the more it hits me just how much baggage she's carrying. Well, I may not be able to make it disappear, but I can help her carry it, if nothing else.

That is, at least, if she will let me.

Chapter 16

It ends up being a bit of a late night, but not nearly as bad as I'd feared. I crawl into bed a little after midnight, which is not ideal on a school night, but I'll survive. Despite the increasing intensity of the situation, I actually feel better than I did earlier in the week. For some reason, the more I try to help Charlotte, the more my own life feels a little less like a dank jail cell. Even the moments that suck, like waking up early after a long night of homework, don't seem quite as awful. Life is just —different.

Before I know it, the week has flown by, and I'm once again entering the ballroom for Swing Dance Club. The day's already gotten off to a much better start than my last visit; I'm on time and have had more than three hours of sleep.

There are the odd cowboy-themed decorations that clash horribly with the more permanent ballroom fixtures. There's the overly peppy music that makes me want to crawl out of my skin. And there, after what has felt like an eternity, is Charlotte. She's leaning against the far wall, brooding. If I didn't know any better, I'd think she was the calmest person in the room. Her eyes lock with mine as I approach her.

I wonder briefly if she's going to push me away, but then she smiles in spite of herself, and just like that, she's okay with me again. I breathe a silent sigh of relief.

"Why did you block me?"

She squirms uncomfortably.

"I probably didn't want to be tempted to call you."

"Probably?"

"My reasoning is getting a little fuzzy for me at this point."

"Well, if you ever do that again when I have something this important to tell you, I'm going to kill you."

"All right," she says demurely. "Wait, important how?"

"There's this sketchy guy who's been asking around for you."

Her eyes go cold.

"His name is--"

"I don't want to know," she breaks in.

"You don't?"

"If I don't know who to hate, it won't be as hard to forgive them."

Interesting way of thinking about it.

"That's noble of you."

She shakes her head.

"I'm no saint. It's just something I've had to learn the hard way."

"Could have fooled me."

"What?"

"Sure, you give off frosty vibes sometimes, but you have a better heart than you let on."

"Wow, what a compliment."

"I'm serious."

She purses her lips.

"How would you know?" she asks, a bit more serious now herself.

"Well, avoiding me because you think you're some sort of walking natural disaster is silly, but that's only because you care about me, right?"

"Care is a strong word."

"You do, though. You care about a lot of things. More than I do, to be honest."

"Then you haven't been around me long enough."

"Then maybe I should start."

She gives me a once-over, face inscrutable.

"I don't get why you're so persistent. Don't you have people to slice open or something?"

"They don't let premed students get within a hundred yards of a scalpel."

"Still. Don't you have anything better to be spending your life on?"

"...No."

A little more emotion trickles into my voice than intended, and Charlotte gives me a different kind of look than I've seen from her before.

"Are you still walking home from campus every day?" I ask.

She gives a little nod.

"Let me walk with you, then. In case that guy shows up again."

"You just can't get enough of me."

"Of course not. Where else am I going to get quality dating advice?"

"I'll think about it," she says, meaning yes.

"Good."

Someone gets up to start the club meeting, and everyone scrambles to find partners for the first dance. Charlotte glances around halfheartedly.

"Well?" I offer.

"All right, then."

I reach up to take her hands, and she doesn't shove mine away.

"You're going to have to help me with the steps," I tell her. "Premed students aren't exactly known for their dancing skills."

"Well, I'm not known for my teaching skills either," she warns. "Let's see, where does the rock step go again? The beginning, I think?"

There's this vulnerable sort of look in her eyes, like I'll accidentally pulverize her heart if I make the wrong move. I'd better watch my step, then.

I'm by no means a natural dancer, so it's all I can do not to crush her toes into oblivion. I manage somehow, but it requires so much focus that I don't have the bandwidth to say much to her. Once the song finishes, we switch partners as instructed, and I continue my struggle to right one of my two left feet. I don't make much progress. Then again, that wasn't really my main purpose for being here anyway.

At the end of the night, Charlotte finds me, and we head out. There's a little chill in the air, but not so much that it's unpleasant. It's overcast enough to obscure most of the stars except for the most persistent among them.

I try to find the words to apologize properly for missing her almost-performance last week, but they don't come.

"Thank you," she says out of nowhere.

"You're welcome."

"I still don't understand why you think I'm worth all this effort."

I try to decide how to phrase it.

"Let's say you were out walking one day and you came across the scene of a crash. No one's around, just you and the driver. Would you call it in?"

"Yes..."

"Even though you just met them?"

"That's different."

"Different how?"

"It's not like my life is on the line."

"Isn't it?"

"I'm not suicidal, you nitwit."

"I didn't say you were. But from the way you talk about music, wouldn't losing it be kind of like dying?"

She's staring down at her hands, like she isn't sure what to do with them.

"Yes," she whispers, surprised. She wasn't expecting me to understand. I don't blame her. To be honest, I'm a little surprised myself.

"Speaking of music, any new singing gigs on the horizon?"

She shakes her head.

"There are a few I'm auditioning for, but I don't know what my chances are."

"It sounds like you're still trying, though."

"For now. There isn't exactly a lot of room up at the top."

"There's always room for the best."

"And how would you know how good I am, screwball?" she says, smiling in spite of herself. "I could be totally tone deaf for all you know."

"*Are* you good?"

"Yes."

"Well, that's how I know." I say with confidence. "I have it on good authority."

"Careful with the sunshine and rainbows, my dude. Any more and I'm going to gag on it."

We chatter on lightheartedly for a few more minutes until we reach her apartment.

"Same time tomorrow?" I suggest as we reach her door."

"I guess." She looks like she wants to say something else, but whatever it is doesn't find its way to her mouth. I want to say something too, but my issue is that I'm not sure exactly what it is.

"I hope at some point you let me in on what you're dealing with," I manage finally.

"I'm dealing with panic attacks."

"I know. You know what I mean."

"I want to leave the past dead and buried, Levi. I don't see the point in digging all that up."

"With all due respect, if the past was really that dead and buried, you wouldn't be struggling this much."

"And how would you know how much I'm struggling?" she snaps.

There's a brief twinge of disappointment in myself as I realize that I've pushed too hard again.

"I don't know," I answer quietly. "Just a hunch."

* * *

I'm a little worried that Charlotte will be angry enough not to show the next day, but my concerns turn out to be unfounded. She texts back as soon as I ask where to meet her and is there waiting for me when I arrive. She doesn't even mention yesterday at all, which is just as well. Sometimes the underside of bridges really is the best place for old water.

Slowly, walking back with her in the evenings becomes part of my new routine. I often find myself mulling over what I want to say to her throughout the day when I should be paying attention to the lectures. There must be some secret combination of words, some magical sauce that will make her panic attacks dissolve into the nothingness from whence they came. That's what therapists do, right?

If there is such a thing, though, I don't succeed in finding it. What I do notice is that my own day begins glowing a bit brighter. There's an extra crispness in the air, an intangible energy that begins to flow even when I'm not actively thinking about Charlotte. The extra time I'm spending on her makes it a little harder to stay on top of my classes, but I find that I don't mind.

Life is good.

Charlotte is a little more closed off than she was before she blocked me. There are times she even shuts down for seemingly no reason, even sometimes when we're talking about mundane things. I can't find a pattern, but I'm sure there is one, even if I can't see it. As a result, I end up walking on eggshells a little more often than I used to.

Even so, I still end up learning more about her, little pieces of things. For example, she's very much a dog person. Every time we pass someone walking one, she cranes her neck to get a better view. Then as soon as we're out of sight, she talks my ear off about the finer points of whatever kind of breed it was and what she likes about it.

"Did you *see* its pointy little ears?" she gushes.

I can't help but smile.

On some topics she is surprisingly insightful. For example, when I told her about the problems I was having talking to Mara (not by name, of course, since apparently there's some kind of bad blood between them), she said:

"If she's so hoity-toity that she can't take a little awkwardness, you're already hosed, buster."

She says it in her normal teasing tone, but she's unironically right. If Mara can get past my social ineptness, I don't have anything to worry about. If she can't, no amount of caution is going to be enough to cover it up.

Charlotte doesn't talk to me much outside of those few minutes every day. Most of my texts go unread for days at a time. But I find myself looking forward to the long walk home more than I ever have.

As the days pass and there's still no sign of Ajay, I begin to hope that my threat of calling the police scared him off and that Charlotte is in the clear now. I don't say anything, though, and neither does Charlotte, so on we go, walking home every day.

Maybe it's wishful thinking on my part, but I swear she's starting to smile more. I take it as a sign that I might not suck at this as much as I thought I did. I know there's still a long way to go, but I can't help but believe in spite of myself that we're on the verge of something great, a mere half-step away from cracking the code that will finally allow Charlotte to let go of the thorns of the past and unleash her inner light.

Chapter 17

A few days later there's another knock at the door. Given what happened last time, my heart rate immediately shoots through the roof. I know the chances of Ajay coming back for another round are slim to none, but I still approach the door with trepidation. On the other side is one of the last people I would have expected.

"Hey, Levi, how's your weekend going?" says Mara.

"Hey, Mara! This is a surprise." I say because it is. Was that a weird thing to say?

"Are you busy tonight?"

"Ah..." I run through a mental checklist of the homework due on Monday. "No, I don't think so."

"Want to go on a date with me?"

"Yes!" I say a slightly too loudly. It makes her smile, though, so that's nice.

"Come on, then."

"*Now?*" Just then I notice she's a bit more dolled up than normal. Wait, what am I wearing again? I look down to check. Sneakers, jeans, a university hoodie. It could be worse, but—"

"Don't worry about it. You already look great," she says, reading my mind. "Come on!"

"All right then."

I follow her out. For some reason, expecting her to walk toward her car. Instead she heads for the sidewalk.

"Wait, we're walking? Don't tell me you don't have a car either?"

She shakes her head.

"Are you kidding me? I'm already going to have to spend half my life paying back student loans! No way am I adding a car payment to that."

"Yeah, for sure," I say, thinking about the mountains of debt I'll likely be in after medical school even with my father's help.

"Besides," she adds, "the place we're going isn't far."

As soon as we step onto the sidewalk, my chest tenses up the way it always does around Mara. My mouth goes dry as I scramble to find something to say.

Calm, I tell myself. *Remember what Charlotte said. If awkwardness was enough to scare her off, she wouldn't have even invited you.*

I take a deep breath. I can do this. Just start a conversation and see what happens. With my mind now clearer, I realize suddenly that I don't really know much about Mara's family.

"Where are you from?"

The words come out a little raspier than I'd have liked, but it's a perfectly serviceable conversation starter.

"From here, actually. I grew up just a few blocks from campus."

If Mara notices just how nervous I am, she doesn't let on. I feel myself start to relax.

"Wow, I didn't know that. But then why are you living in an apartment instead of with family?"

She shrugs.

"I just felt like I needed my own space. My parents are wonderful, but they can be a bit...smothering sometimes."

I thought of phone calls with my dad. How much worse would it be if I *lived* with him. I shudder at the thought.

"You, too, it looks like," she chuckles.

"Probably not in the same way as your parents, but yeah."

We chatter on like that for a while. *I'm doing it,* I realize with a shock. *I'm actually stringing coherent thoughts together on the fly.* Not only that, but the conversation is actually *flowing.*

"Hey, sorry you had to be the one to make the first move," I say apologetically. "I've been meaning to ask you out for a while but it just never happened."

"Well, you can fix that next time." She gives me a look that makes my heart skip a beat. Then I see the sign for the Ice Palace and my heart skips another beat, this time for a completely unrelated reason. I'd been so engrossed in the conversation that I didn't fully realize where we're headed until we are already in the parking lot. My stomach sinks and ties itself into a Gordian knot so tight, even Alexander couldn't untangle it. You see, I have no idea how to ice skate.

"This place is great," Mara chatters on. "I used to come here all the time when I was younger."

"Yeah, great," I manage. My dialogue generator is whining under the strain of my new mental load. This is bad.

We make our way inside. At the ticket counter is a twenty-something-year-old with the largest beard I've ever seen on a college student standing in the entryway. His eyes light up as we approach.

"What up, Mara! You finally came while I was on shift! Slay, girl! Drink that heavenly fire, babe!"

He steps around the corner and gives her a quick hug, then turns to me.

"What up, bro! I hope you're ready to vibe tonight." He hugs me as well. That only serves to put me even more on edge.

I open my mouth to spill the beans to Mara, as there's no use trying to hide my lack of skill since it will be painfully obvious as soon as we step onto the ice. The problem is that Beard Guy doesn't let me get a word in edgewise.

"Come along, my dude. I'll get you sorted. Did you catch the game yesterday? How about those Mammoths, am I right? Well, there's always next year, I guess. It seems like I say that earlier and earlier every season. But I hear the recruiting class is supposed to be a lot better. Nice weather, though. I think it's supposed to get chillier in a couple of weeks. Not looking forward to that. Anyways, what size skates can I get you?"

"Nine," I say, hoping it's about the same as normal shoe sizes.

Beard Guy whips out an appropriate set of skates and slings them toward me. Then he's off racing to get Mara outfitted, chattering on about the latest shows. I don't understand people like him. How is it possible to have such an unending list of things to talk about? Here I am struggling to fill five minutes. He ushers us into the rink area, where I prepare to meet my doom. We sit down on a bench to put on our skates. There aren't many people here today, which is a good thing as far as I'm concerned. Fewer people to watch my inevitable demise. A couple of them are kids that can't be any older than six or seven, skating around the rink like they were born that way. That eases my anxiety a little bit. If children can do it that easily, it must not be too hard, right? Maybe I'll be a natural.

The second I try to stand up with my skates on, all that positivity goes out the window. My feet slide out in opposite directions, and I have to catch myself on the short wall between the benches and the actual rink. This...is not going to end well. I glance surreptitiously over at Mara. She doesn't seem to have noticed yet.

"By the way--"

"What are we waiting for?" she cuts in. "Let's get out there!"

She grabs my hand, and my mind goes blank at the worst possible moment. I try to stand again without thinking, and this time I'm not fast enough to catch myself.

Wham! I slam into Mara. Not in the cutesy, romantic comedy way, but in the bone-crushing, concussion-threatening way.

"Ack!"

She topples back onto the bench, grabbing at the wall to catch herself. I lean back in the opposite direction in an effort not to fall on top of her and end up careening the other way, windmilling my arms like a deranged monkey. I plant a bladed foot behind me in an effort to stop myself, but it slides out from under me and sends me into a frantic tap dance to keep me upright. That lasts all of three seconds before I overbalance once more and crash headlong into the wall. I lean against it, gingerly reaching for the back of the bench to steady myself in case my legs give way again. Mara pulls herself to her feet.

"Did I bump you? Sorry. I'm such a klutz."

"That isn't it," I force out. "I just--"

She reaches for my hand again.

"I won't do it again, I promise."

"Actually—"

She grabs my hand a second time. I lean away from her reflexively and get out of balance almost immediately, sending me into another tap dance. I let go of her hand, determined not to take her down with me this time. After some frantic scrambling, I manage to get over to the short wall surrounding the rink and brace myself against it.

"Are you okay?"

"Does it look like I'm okay? I've never been skating before!" I get out finally.

As I'm standing there, my legs slide too far apart, and I'm back to the tap dance again. Mara has a hand over her face, choking down a laugh. My face is redder than a strawberry dowsed in ketchup fondue.

"Um, well, maybe with some practice?"

It's a minor miracle that I'm able to get out onto the ice at all. I almost fall a half dozen times. Finally I manage it, stumbling haphazardly onto the rink and then clinging to the outside wall for dear life.

"Don't be so afraid of it!" says Mara, skating by me going backwards. "Just push yourself forward a little at a time."

I try this, letting go of the wall against my better judgment and striking out around the rink. I last all of four seconds before my skates slide out from under me and, not having anything to hang onto this time, I hit the ground hard.

Not to be deterred, I haul myself to my feet and try again. This time I last even less time before pile driving into the ground yet again. One of the kids I'd seen earlier whizzes by me with a pitying look on her face. I want to crawl into a deep dark hole and never be seen again. So much for making a good impression on Mara. I've never seen someone try so hard not to laugh.

I give up on striking out into the middle and clutch the wall with one hand, making my way slowly around the outside. Meanwhile, Mara is skating lap after lap around the rink, shouting encouraging words every time she goes past. Some date this turned out to be. I'm beginning to regret ever having the gall to believe that I could handle this romance stuff. I should have just given it up from the start and consigned myself to a life of being single.

"Hey, we don't have to keep doing this," she says after the tenth time I hit the deck. The fact that I'm so relieved by her saying that only drives my embarrassment ever deeper.

"Yeah, that's a good idea."

I slowly make my way around to the exit, hating every moment with a burning passion. Mara helps me back over to a bench to change out of our skates with less than half the dignity I started with.

I sit, deeply grateful to be attached to a non-slippery surface once more.

"You weren't kidding when you said you'd never done this before," says Mara.

"Yeah."

I unlace one of my skates. As I do so, I notice a stinging sensation in my foot.

"Those look way too loose," says Mara. "Did you get them in your shoe size instead of your skate size?"

The defeated look on my face speaks for itself. I'm so caught up in the chafing from having worn skates that were too big that I don't notice my feet sliding away from me again. I have to catch myself on the bench, narrowly avoiding the most embarrassing tumble of them all.

"Did you just--" Mara is in laugh-stifling mode again. "Did you just almost fall while *sitting--*"

I don't know why that comment in particular hurts so much. If, for example, Charlotte were here, she'd be tearing into me even worse, and I wouldn't even bat an eye. But it does hurt, coming from her. I rip off my skates as fast as humanly possible, as the physical pain now pales in comparison to the emotional variety. I understand now why Charlotte always looks away when I ask her uncomfortable questions.

"You're bleeding!"

I look down to see that she's right. The chafing is so bad that in places there are little droplets of blood soaking through my socks. It's not enough to warrant a band-aid, though, so I just tug on my shoes and book it out of there as fast as humanly possible.

"Short skate tonight," says Beard Guy.

I don't answer. I know I'm being rude, but I just can't right now. Mara ushers me out the door, clearly recognizing this. It closes behind us with vicious finality, locking the miry details of my humiliation here today forever into the annals of the past.

Chapter 18

The breath of air I take outside the rink has to be simultaneously the most disgusting and the most succulent I've ever tasted. Mara is absolutely crestfallen. Understandably so. She'd been looking forward to skating at a place from her childhood, and because of me, she was only able to be there for a few minutes.

"I'm sorry."

She doesn't say anything at first, just keeps walking. I guess I've blown my chance with her. That's just as well. It was silly to think I ever had more than a teaspoonful of hope to start with.

"It's okay," Mara says finally.

That makes me feel a little better, but I'm not sure if she actually means it.

We've arrived at a park. I'm not really sure if we've ended up here randomly, or if Mara steered us here on purpose. We start onto a trail that encircles the park. It feels good to be on solid ground again, but I doubt Mara feels the same.

We walk on in silence for a while. Eventually we happen upon a little gazebo. Mara goes to sit down, and I follow her lead. Part of me wants this date to be over already, and another part of me is curious why it doesn't seem to be heading in that direction yet.

"I'm sorry," I say again, because it's the only thing I can think to say. "It feels like I'm always stepping in it around you."

"To be honest," Mara says finally, "I'm also upset with myself."

"What? Why?" I look up at her, surprised.

"I dragged you into something that made you really uncomfortable. This is the kind of thing I go for, and I guess I just assumed that you would too. *I'm* the one screwing everything up all the time. Like how I wouldn't help you with that stalker thing because I was jealous and because of my history with Charlotte."

The revelations are coming too fast for me to keep up. Jealous? History with Charlotte? Does that mean they knew each other before college?

"Knowing her background, I don't really know how you could go for someone like her, but I also kind of feel like I'm never going to measure up in your eyes."

She doesn't think she measures up in *my* eyes?

"With Charlotte, it's kind of a different thing than you think," I explain. "I'm just trying to help her out. I mean, I do care about her," Mara gives me a look. "But it's different. It's not like I want to kiss her or anything."

Mara's face is suddenly much closer to me than it was before. Her peach lip balm glistens under the light of the nearby streetlamps

"Is that so?" she says quietly. "You're so cute sometimes, Levi."

My brain can't compute what's happening. Cute? Me? How is that possible? My heart pounds like a jackhammer as my whole being threatens to be swallowed up in her beautiful, glistening eyes.

"You can be so dense sometimes. But I can never help myself from coming closer even though I know I might get burned."

"Oh yeah?" I say, not sure if that's a good thing or a bad thing but mostly overwhelmed by how close she's getting, "Why's that?"

"Because I like you too much."

Her lips brush mine, and a firework explodes in my brain. All other thoughts fall out of both of our heads. Another firework hits, and then another. Then my phone starts going off, and I pull back slightly.

I'm not about to check it; even I can tell that would be a disaster. But now suddenly I'm so self-conscious that I can't stand it.

"I don't know why in the world you'd still be interested in me after I just embarrassed you so badly."

"I guess you're not the only dumb one," she says fondly.

"Next time *I'll* be the one to ask *you* out."

"Yeah, you will." For some reason that suddenly seems like the funniest thing in the world, and I break down laughing.

"What?"

"You're really not going to cut me any slack, are you?"

"No," she says playfully, tracing the back of my hand with a finger, "because I think you're going to live up to my expectations." She stands, which I take as a cue that it's time to go.

"Shall I walk you home?" I manage. "I'm the same direction, I think."

"My, what a gentleman."

Mara smiles at me in a way that makes me melt inside, but also shrink away from her as far as humanly possible. There's something strangely uncomfortable about this.

I suddenly remember Charlotte's advice.

"What kinds of dates do you like?"

Mara gives me a long look, a sliver of a smile tickling the edge of her mouth.

"Surprise me."

It's not really an answer, but somehow it tells me everything I need to know.

When we reach her door, Mara gives me a quick peck on the lips and disappears inside with a look that gives me goosebumps for all the right reasons. I let out a long breath that I didn't realize I'd been holding. The last half of that date was everything I'd hoped and dreamed, but somehow it feels so *weird* now that it's reality. Aren't I supposed to be happy right now? I mean, I guess I am, kind of. There's this surge of euphoria that makes my skin tingle, but there's kind of an odd almost sickening quality to it that I can't place. I want to cheer and hurl at the same time.

Wait, what was that call from earlier? I pull out my phone and do a double take. It was Charlotte.

She never calls. Ever. The butterflies that had been aflutter in my stomach take a hit from some particularly nasty bug spray. I hit the green Call button and jerk the phone up to my ear. Of course, now she's not going to answer again, and I'm going to be livid with myself for missing her.

"Hello?"

"Charlotte!"

"Oh...hi..."

"Charlotte, what is going on?"

"Agh. I was going to...but now I think it's a bad idea..."

"What? Spit it out!"

"Never mind."

I pound the side of the building next to me.

"Whatever it is, it's going to be okay, so *just tell me already.*"

"It's been a rough evening."

"You and me both."

She goes quiet.

"*So...?*" I supply

"I don't think I can tell you. I was going to, but--"

"But what?"

"I don't think I'm ready."

I let out a little groan. Wait, could she hear that?

"I'm sorry, I know I'm a bit much to put up with."

She heard. I die a little inside.

"Put up with—you know I *wanted* you to call me, right?"

"You're such a nice person, Levi. You really don't have to lie to me."

"*I'm not lying to you!*"

"Don't let my warped brain wear off on you."

"Are you not hearing a single word I'm saying?"

"Have a good night, Levi."

I slam my head against the wall repeatedly, unsure whether it was worse to have a phone call like that with her or none at all.

"That sounded fun." I whirl around.

"Eavesdropping is rude." I spit out with as much vehemence as I can squeeze into my voice.

"It sounds like you're not the only one lying to yourself," says Micah. He has his backpack on and is standing in the threshold of the door to our apartment.

The fact that he was eavesdropping, not only on me but also Charlotte, really gets my blood boiling. She must have been speaking loudly enough for him to pick up the gist of her side of the conversation as well.

"Ever heard of personal space?"

"You aren't trying to be a therapist, are you?" he queries, ignoring the question.

"You're seriously going to butt into someone else's personal mental health challenges?"

"At least I'm not prying into things I don't have the qualifications to mess with. Knowing you, you're going to

come in swinging and leave her more messed up than she
is already."

I almost hit him. I honestly don't know what stops
me. It's certainly not the fear of him using Nietzsche to
pummel me into oblivion. It'd be awfully difficult to
quote Nietzsche with a few less teeth than he started the
day with.

Instead, I snap, "Takes one to know one," and take
off down the street. There's no way I'm coming back
before midnight. I am *not* going to deal with him today. I
don't care if he looks down on me for it.

I make my way toward campus with no idea what
I'm going to do when I get there. I took off without any
of my school supplies, but it's not like I'm going to get
any homework done in this state of mind anyway. I just
need the roller coaster to slow down a second so I can
get my head screwed on straight.

I am absolutely wired from my date earlier. It's not
like I don't want Mara to like me, but I do wish that the
sheer nervous energy it's sending through me would chill
out a half step.

And then there's Charlotte. What's with her today?
In some ways I know her so well, but in others I feel like
I'm barely starting to understand. She seems to want to
open up to me more, but there's something getting in the
way that neither of us seems to be able to put a finger on.
Although I certainly didn't make it any easier by making
her think that I was annoyed at her.

*You're going to come in swinging and leave her more
messed up than she was already,* Inner Micah chimes in
with his most nasally, most obnoxious voice. I wish I
could run away from him as well.

After a few more minutes of walking, my head clears
somewhat. Charlotte did actually call me for once. That's
something. On the other hand, if I'd been there to
answer her first call instead of being buried knee-deep in

my own hormones, she probably would have come out with it. Now instead of knowing how to help her, the door to the deeper levels of her heart is still firmly locked and bolted.

I go to kick a random rock on the sidewalk and miss completely. Somehow it feels like the perfect metaphor for my life right now. If someone had told me twenty-four hours ago that I was going to go on a date with Mara and get closer to rebuilding trust with Charlotte, I would have been over the moon. Right now all I feel is emptiness and failure. Why does the path forward seem so murky?

My phone vibrates, and I nearly jump out of my skin. It's Mara.

`I had fun today :)`

My heart sings despite itself. Maybe the date wasn't such a bad idea after all.

Chapter 19

I text back and forth with Mara quite a bit over the first part of the week. I like talking to her this way much better than face-to-face because I can take my time thinking through what to say back. For her part, she responds quickly and generally seems happy to hear from me. Not about to make the same mistake twice, I push through my wall of nerves and ask her on a date for next Friday. I shouldn't be surprised that she says yes, but somehow I still am.

What are we doing?

I thought you told me to
surprise you.

:P

Tongue sticking out emoji. Nice. I'm so absorbed with my blossoming...relationship?...almost relationship? that before I know it, the week has flown by, and it's time for Swing Dance Club once more. I've had to miss the last couple of weeks because I had exams to study for, but I've been practicing enough on my own that I'm much less likely to endanger anyone else's feet this time around. I look around for Charlotte and spot her almost immediately in her usual place near the far wall.

Excellent. She's been quiet on our walks home lately. Hopefully this will be a good opportunity to weasel out what's been bothering her.

I make my way toward her.

"Levi!" Someone's calling my name, but whoever it is can wait. I make eye contact with Charlotte, and an expression that I can't interpret flashes across her face. Maybe a hint of a smile? She's wearing her brown contacts today for some reason. She does that sometimes, but there doesn't seem to be any pattern to when or why. She still won't tell me why she has them.

Someone grabs my shoulder so hard it stops me dead in my tracks.

"Levi! I'm right here!" I turn reluctantly to find Mara staring at me in that penetrating way she does. Instantly I know that I'm hosed. Somehow it entirely slipped my mind that she goes to this club too. Luckily, she seems to think that she's the one I was trying to find. If she knew that Charlotte was the first one on my mind today, I don't even want to think about the wrath that would ensue.

"Care to dance?" I say, turning away from Charlotte with a soft sting of regret.

Mara shows me the basic dance moves, not realizing Charlotte already beat her to it. I'm too distracted to concentrate.

"Add a rock step at the *end*. Did you leave your ears at home or something?

"Sorry. You make it hard to focus," my mouth says before I can stop it."Well, if it's for that reason..." Mara says, cheeks flushed. "And now you spin me around the other way and hold me close."

My insides melt into a puddle of goo. On the other side of the ballroom Charlotte is dancing with a guy with biceps the size of France. She seems a little out of it. I eye her worriedly. Is she eating enough?

"Now you dip me," says Mara. I snap back into focus and dip her hurriedly, letting her down a bit too fast.

"Careful! Valuable merchandise!"

"Sorry."

I stumble my way through a couple more songs. I can tell Mara's getting frustrated, but she's doing her best to hide it.

Then the song ends, and the announcer says:

"Time to switch partners!"

"Looks like we have to switch," I say with a frown, stepping away. She looks a little relieved, and I can't blame her. I scan the crowd for a new partner, shoulders tensing. My eyes naturally find their way to Charlotte, who is wandering this way. She looks over at me and gives her head a questioning tilt. I take a couple steps toward her but then think better of it. Mara probably wouldn't be a fan of me dancing with her. I quickly pivot, and I ask the girl closest to me.

"The rock step is at the end," my new partner reminds me.

"Ah, yes. Thanks."

I'm still awfully out of it today. It's all I can do to pay enough attention to the girl in front of me not to be impolite.

"You're new at this, aren't you?"

"Yeah. I've practiced a bit, but I'm still pretty--,"

I freeze. There, standing by the far wall in almost the exact spot Charlotte was at the beginning of club, is Ajay. His face is more grizzled than I when I last saw him, and there's something about him that's harder. Angrier. I strongly suspect that he isn't here to dance.

Where's Charlotte? It takes me a minute to find her again. Fortunately she's on the opposite end of the room from him, so we should be safe for now. The trick will be getting over there without alerting Ajay. I try to steer my partner a little closer, but it's awfully difficult when I keep forgetting what I'm supposed to be doing half the time. Finally, I realize it's just not working.

"Sorry, I have to go," I tell my partner. She looks minorly offended, and I feel bad, but there's nothing I can do about it. I've got to get Charlotte out of here before Ajay makes his move, whatever it is.

Speaking of Ajay, he's still staring into the crowd, looking at faces one by one. Fortunately, there are a lot more people here than there were at the beginning, but it's still only a matter of time before he finds her. Her brown contacts might help a bit, but we can't count on it.

I'm halfway to her when the song stops, and the scramble to find a new partner begins again. I glance back at Ajay to keep tabs on him, but he suddenly isn't there. Not good. I speed up, on high alert now. Surely he wouldn't try something with so many people around. Still, there has to be a reason he's here.

I'm only about twenty yards from Charlotte now. She's got a concerned look on her face, although it's not clear why. I take a few more steps toward her, and then the music starts again, and a nerdy-looking kid with glasses snaps her up.

I have to be quick, or I'll stand out like a sore thumb. The remaining distance dissolves before me at a speedwalk, and I grab her hand, pulling it away from her partner. Her eyes go wide as she looks up.

"I'm going to have to borrow her, sorry."

Her eyes flash. She lets go of her partner's other hand and lets me lead her away without the sarcastic jab I'm expecting. I grab her hands like I'm dancing with her. Which I guess technically I am.

"That guy that was creeping around asking about you is here."

A ripple of emotions crosses her face. She sets her jaw and swallows slowly.

"About time you asked me to dance," she tells me, hands griping mine far too tightly.

"About time you let me."

"But last club meeting we also—oh." She sees the look on my face. "Yeah, I guess so."

"We should get out of here."

"Sure."

I move to lead her off of the dance floor, but then she stops. I look at her.

"If you have to decide between what makes sense and what feels right, what do you do?" she asks.

"Is there ever a reason to do something that doesn't make sense?"

She looks at me. Really looks at me.

"I think....that I don't want to run anymore."

She takes two steps and spins me. It takes me off-guard, but I manage keep my balance. I finish the turn and flow into leading her through a spin of her own. What exactly is she doing? I get the rock step wrong again, but suddenly she adjusts her tempo to meet mine, and it's almost like it's been right all along.

"This is nice and all, but--"

Charlotte rolls along my back, pulling my arm up over her head and twisting into a modified cuddle position. I'm not sure what's going on here, but there's something about it that feels *right* somehow.

We step and spin and twirl and dip. Reality falls away. The only thing in all of existence is her. Her and the moment. Why she would choose now of all times to do this I can't fathom. But maybe it's the sheer incomprehensibility of it that makes the moment somehow reach deeper than the brush of her hand against mine. She's called, and eternity itself has answered. I hope that one day it will answer me, too.

Each movement flows into the next in an unending kaleidoscope of motion and rhythm. Each step is unlikely to impress an expert, but to us, who don't know the difference, it feels right, feels perfect.

And then the moment ends. We reach the entrance to the ballroom without even having tried and duck around the corner, sides heaving. We share a look.

Whatever just happened is too special to ruin by speaking the obvious.

"It's good to have you back," I tell her.

"It's good to be back."

I grab her hand instinctively and lead her out of the building and several hundred yards away, where it feels safer. I shiver. There's been a cold snap this week, which means there are now fewer people wandering around outside who might overhear us. Ajay is nowhere to be seen. We've lost him.

"So why is someone stalking you? You never seemed surprised by that."

"I'm just so popular that people can't help themselves."

"Charlotte."

"I hope I don't get any fan mail. It would be a real pain answering it all."

"Charlotte."

"You'd have to help reply to some of it, and I'd have to watch you closely so you didn't crush some little girl's dreams."

"Charlotte."

She stops and bends over, sides heaving for reasons unrelated to physical exertion. The doors to her heart, which have been kicked wide open by the dancing, start to close again.

"No! Don't you shut down on me."

She tries, she really does, but she's fighting a losing battle. I sigh.

"It's okay. You can tell me when you're ready."

She stares off into the distance. Suddenly her eyes sharpen with a determination I've never seen in them before.

"I screwed up a long time ago, and there are a lot of people who are still mad about it."

She says the words slowly and deliberately, as if she has to squeeze a drop of blood into each one as the admission price. I consider my response carefully. It's imperative that I handle this right.

"They're so mad...that they're coming after you?"

"It was a major screw up."

"What? You spiked someone's orange juice with hot sauce or something?"

She doesn't laugh.

"You know I'm not going to ditch you regardless of what it is, right?"

Slow nod.

"I'm not going to abandon you."

Another nod. She's closed up almost completely now, but for some reason, I can still sense some of what's going on beneath the surface.

"Will you at least come talk to the police with me? If you give them some background, they might be more willing to--"

"No!"

"Why not?"

"I don't like the police."

I want to push further, but I'm treading on thin ice here. Well, if she won't do that--

"If you see anyone suspicious hanging around your apartment you call me, okay?"

No response.

"Okay?"

She nods slowly, eyes glassy. I take her face in my hands, trying to get her to focus.

Her eyes gradually lock onto mine.

"You'll call me if you see anyone suspicious following you, right?"

"Sure."

She takes a deep breath. Then a deeper one.

"So the mistake I made was--"

I hear footsteps and pull back quickly, suddenly self-conscious. I hadn't meant anything by holding her head like that, and it did seem to help Charlotte come back to Earth, but anyone watching would definitely not see it that way.

"Levi!"

It's Mara. I momentarily have a spike of pure terror before remembering that I told her about the stalker before. Good, maybe she can help.

"Charlotte's stalker was at the club meeting," I say quickly. "I was just telling her to call me if he shows up again, but maybe if she can get your number too..." I trail off. Mara is giving Charlotte a look of such hostility I'm surprised the pavement she's standing on doesn't ignite.

"It's true! I swear!"

Mara calls Charlotte something best left unrepeated, and now I'm back to freaking out again.

"I'm not lying!"

Mara's gaze flicks to mine.

"I know you're not lying, Levi."

Then why...I look back over at Charlotte to see that she's flattened herself against the wall of the building behind her and seems to be trying to squeeze herself into the mortar. The terror is gone again, replaced by complete confusion.

"What's going on here?"

Neither of them answer, so I step in front of Charlotte like a human shield.

"Can't you just let whatever it is go?"

"No." Mara doesn't provide any further explanation, so I look back over at Charlotte. She's starting to shake.

My heart sinks. No! Not right now! Not when she was so close to letting me in! As I watch on helplessly, the seriousness of the situation becomes clear. At the very moment Charlotte's gathered the courage to tell me what's really going on, she's being plunged ruthlessly into the throes of a panic attack.

Chapter 20

Panic attack incoming. Of all the awful timing!

"Well, whatever it is, it's going to have to wait," I tell Mara. I grab Charlotte by the shoulder, which is the most platonic approach I can come up with under the watchful gaze of my potential soon-to-be girlfriend, and steer her down the walkway. She follows numbly.

"I'll call you later!" I yell back to Mara. She lets us go without comment.

As soon as we're away, I sit Charlotte down on a bench and wait for the shaking to subside. It's a little less intense this time, possibly because I got her out of the situation so quickly. It's only about a minute or so before she's mostly lucid again. I breathe a sigh of relief.

"Let's get you home, yes?"

"As long as it's you that's asking."

Charlotte's still looking a little out of it. She doesn't live far, but I'm still a little nervous about making her walk.

"Are you going to make it on foot?"

"My car's in the student parking garage."

Wait, car?

"You got it fixed? But you've still been walking with me every day!"

Her eyes are glued to her shoes. I want to pry further, but she has that fragile sort of look she does that pulls me up short. There will be time for that later.

After forever and a day of climbing stairs into the depths of the parking garage, Charlotte leads me over to a very familiar-looking gray coupe with black trim.

"Are you okay to drive?" I ask.

"Marvelous."

I hold my hand out for the keys and tell her to get in. The steering wheel is ice cold, making my hands go numb.

When we're finally on the road and after an intense internal debate, I finally proffer the question she must have known was coming.

"What's with you and Mara?"

"Mara?"

"That girl that was mad at you."

Which Mara did she think I meant?

"Oh, her. I did something really bad to her a long time ago." The words again come slowly and painfully. There's no way for me to take away the sting of it, and even if I could, it feels like doing so would cheapen it somehow. There are no shortcuts on the path she walks.

"At some point, do you think you'll forgive yourself?"

"Kind of hard to do that when people still hate my guts for it."

"I don't hate your guts."

"You don't count. You'd be cheering me on if I was on death row."

"That's the point."

An odd look comes over her face, and she falls silent. Not sure what to say at this point, I distract myself by studying the intricacies of the panda key chain dangling from the rear-view mirror.

"Thanks for saving me," she says.

"I'm glad you see it that way."

"How else would I see it?"

"Like I just shoved my nose somewhere it didn't belong."

"Don't you remember what I told you on our date, Levi?"

I look over at her.

"Even your mistakes are perfect."

"I'm pretty sure that's not how you phrased it last time."

"Well, it's true."

"So I did make a mistake asking about you and Mara."

"I wouldn't say that. Just because I don't like it doesn't mean it's not helping."

"Well, I'm glad I didn't screw it up too badly," and then, as much to myself as to her, "I'm not going to let my own selfishness get in the way of being there when you need me."

"Please don't."

"What?"

"I don't want something else to feel guilty about."

"With all due respect," I say with a certain fondness, "it's not up to you."

I instantly regret the forceful response and expect her to immediately crumple again, but to my surprise she doesn't.

"Yeah, yeah, yeah."

It isn't until I pull into the parking lot of her apartment complex that I notice that her back seat is still covered in sheet music.

"Still breathing this stuff, I see."

"Always."

"You should sing for me sometime."

"...Maybe."

"You were going to sing at Swing Dance Club, right? So what's the difference?" I ask, pulling into a parking space.

"Because...mumble mumble...special." she says too quietly for me to make out.

"What?"

"Nothing."

We get to her door. She's breathing at a normal rate now but otherwise looks like she's run a marathon. I'm still a little worried, but I doubt she wants to see much more of me today.

"Call me if you need me."

"Sure."

"Promise?"

"Aye aye, Captain."

"Well, see you around."

I turn to go back down the steps. Then I stop. Because Charlotte has just thrown her arms around my middle.

"Please don't go," she says so quietly I almost can't hear her.

"Sure."

She has a hard time making eye contact with me as I follow her inside. She's embarrassed.

Once I get through the door, it's obvious why. I wasn't exactly expecting a palace based on the outside, but the dwelling I step into is almost not habitable. The couch has a gigantic gash in it running along the outside, and there's almost no other furniture, at least not in the front room. There's drywall missing in places. And everything in sight is covered in a light layer of tiny unidentifiable brown things.

"What are they?" I ask.

"Termites."

What? I look closer and see that they are actually wings. Do termites even have wings?

"Where do they come from?"

She points up.

"In the ceiling somewhere. They've gotten a little quieter since it's gotten colder, but still--" As she says this, a couple more wings flutter down onto the sofa to illustrate her point.

"Is this...legal?"

She shrugs.

"We've been on the landlord's case about it since we've been here. He said he did something about it, but whatever it was obviously didn't work."

I'd spent lot of time trying to picture what the inside of this place looked like. The reality was worse than anything I'd imagined. Charlotte still won't look at me.

"Hey, don't be like that. I happened to be hankering to hang out in a girl's apartment just now."

"Yeah, yeah, don't get too comfortable. Next time I'm going to charge admission."

"Thanks for letting me in," I say, meaning this in two ways at once.

Her eyes drift up to mine.

I brace myself for her to brush me off and shut down again, but instead she shocks me completely by collapsing into me.

"Don't get full of yourself. I just don't want to be alone right now."

"Well, feel free to be not alone next to me."

Her apartment is so horribly, horribly desolate. Even turning all the lights on doesn't seem to help much. It's awfully chilly.

"Are your roommates morticians or something?"

"What?"

"It's gloomy enough for a funeral in here."

"'Course not. It's hard to be a mortician if you're already dead inside."

We brush the termite wings off the couch and sit down. I look down at Charlotte, whose head is now on my shoulder. Physical contact like this feels so natural, for some reason, like it shouldn't even mean anything particularly significant. But it's a sign that she's starting to trust me, and that's worth more to me than any amount of money.

"Charlotte, what were you going to tell me when you called last week?" I ask, because there's a chance she might actually tell me right now.

"I really, really hate being alone," she says, half answering.

"So you kept pushing me away? I get that you think that you're going to mess up my life somehow, but I don't care. Let it get messed up."

"You'd rather be here than with what's-her-name...Mara?"

I hesitate to reply, not because I'm unsure of the answer, but because it seems like it's not the one I'm supposed to give. Mara and I are practically dating now. If I say I'd rather be here, wouldn't that imply--

Too late I realize that Charlotte is interpreting my hesitation in the opposite direction. She shoves away from me, curling into a ball as far away from me as possible.

"Charlotte--"

"Stay away from me!" She hurls a dirty sock in my direction. I realize with a sinking heart that there's nothing I can say now that will make it better, no expression of affection or loyalty that she won't see as pity in disguise. Denying it will make it worse. Defending myself will make it worse. So instead, I just sit there in silence, wishing I could cry. I wait, for what I can't say.

Eventually she unwraps herself from her fetal position but remains an arm's length away.

"I just want you to be okay," I tell her finally.

"I don't believe you," she says, leaning her head on my shoulder again, shivering involuntarily.

"Seriously, how low are you guys keeping the thermostat in here?"

"Um..."

Then it hits me.

"Did they turn your heat off?"

Her silence tells me all I need to know.

"How long has it been off? It's supposed to get below freezing next week!"

"I guess we'll just have to keep warm by the light of our hopes and dreams."

"Seriously!"

"What do you want me to say? We're out of money. Is that a crime, or something? Don't worry about it. We have propane space heaters."

The conversation trails off. I stay there until I hear her breathing get deep and heavy. She doesn't wake up even when I shift her head over to one of the couch cushions. As I look down at her, a certain heaviness settles over my shoulders. I brush away a couple of termite wings that have settled in her hair. *Seriously!* How is it okay for human beings to have to live like this?

I manage to find one of the space heaters she talked about and turn it on. It's an inefficient way of heating a room like this, but at least this way she won't freeze. Then I stand and let myself out, being sure to lock the doorknob on the way out in case Ajay is lurking around a corner somewhere. After his shenanigans today, it wouldn't surprise me.

It's pitch black outside. I still have some homework to finish for tomorrow, so it's going to be a late night. I don't care. This is more important. The thought of how cold that apartment is going to get next week turns my stomach. I have to figure out a way to help with that. Now that I have a better idea of what her living conditions are, I can't help but be amazed by Charlotte. How much would my GPA be suffering if I had to live in that anthill of an apartment? Yet she does it like it's nothing.

I am a bit concerned that Charlotte may be falling for me, though, based on her reaction earlier.

You're going to mess her up more than she already is, chimes in my Inner Micah again. What if letting her glom onto me somehow winds up making her mental health worse? As much as I'm loath to admit it, Micah is right about this one: I'm not a professional therapist. What am I supposed to do about panic attacks? Or termites?

It occurs to me that I could really use Mason's advice right now. Then it occurs to me that maybe it's possible for me to get it right now if I'm determined enough.

As soon as I get home, I knock on his door. No answer. That's expected. I've only ever seen him here late at night. Well, that's just as well since I have homework to finish anyway. I muddle my way through some Comparative Literature reading, being careful not to drift off. It would be just my luck to fall asleep right before he gets here.

I finish the assignment, but he still isn't back, so I start studying for my next Biology exam. I spend another half hour on that, but still no Mason. I get ready for bed, ears peeled for the sound of the door opening. No Mason. I eat a can of peaches because I haven't really had a proper dinner. He's still not here. I scroll through social media and watch some random videos online. Am I really prepared to stick this out?

I can feel myself fading, so I sit directly in front of Mason's door. I'm in over my head here, and as much as I want to limit the number of people who know about Charlotte's personal struggles, I'm not going to be able to figure out the right answer on my own. This is the only

way I can think of to get the answers I so desperately
need.

* * *

I'm not exactly sure when I drift off, but it's the door
shutting hard that snaps me awake again. I blink blearily.
Mason is staring down at me. If it was anyone else, I'd be
rather embarrassed, but he's not the type to judge.

"Hard time sleeping?"

I blink a few more times, trying to parse what he's
just said. Finally it clicks and I stand up.

"I need some advice."

"Your friend with panic attacks again?"

"Yes."

He sits down at the kitchen table and motions
toward a nearby chair. I can't help but notice the bags
under his eyes, but he doesn't seem at all bothered by my
question.

"I'm all ears."

I sit down.

"How do I know I'm not making things worse by
trying to help her?"

He smiles at that.

"That's such a relatable question. I used to worry
about that when I first became a therapist. The truth is
that it's a lot harder to mess these things up than you
might think."

That wasn't what I was expecting.

"Really?"

"Don't get me wrong, I'm not telling you to try to be
her therapist," he quickly clarifies. "And you do need to
be a little careful not to go digging into the details of her
past trauma. If she's not ready to go there, that really *can*
cause damage. Honestly, though, one of the saddest
things I hear is when someone I work with tries to

confide in a friend or family member only to be told 'go tell your therapist about that.' The truth is, as long as you're respectful and compassionate, you're doing just fine. In fact, in some ways you can help her more than a therapist can."

That's a weird thing to hear coming from him.

"What do you mean?'

"There are certain things that I can do as a therapist that I can't in my private life, like hashing out the details of someone else's trauma and using therapy techniques to help them break the cycle of emotional avoidance. There are also things I can't do that you can, like lending someone money or spending all day with them when they're struggling. I only see people once a week, so it's a lot less likely that I'll be there at the moments when they need someone the most."

"So I'm not going to mess everything up?"

"Nothing is guaranteed, but based on how you've been talking about your friend, I can tell that you care about her a lot. I assume that you're not going to tell her to 'just get over it' or blow her off if she wants to confide in you?"

"Never."

"Then I'm not worried."

"Oh. Okay."

A vote of confidence was not exactly what I was expecting.

"How do I handle it if she has another panic attack?"

"The important thing is not to panic yourself and feed into it. If you're calm, and she can sense that, it will help her feel safe and potentially resolve the situation quicker. It might also help to direct her attention to one of the five senses to help ground her to the present moment, like noticing a particular noise or paying attention to her breathing."

"That sounds way too simple."

"A lot of things that actually work really are simple. But simple doesn't necessarily mean easy. If it did, I'd probably be out of a job."

Mason gives a deep chuckle that trails off at the end.

"All right, thanks for the advice."

"Of course. Although next time you should just text me so you don't have to wait up for me so long. Here's my number."

He hands it to me on a sticky note.

"Thanks," I say, feeling a bit dumb for not thinking of that sooner. It sounds like I need to be careful not to push Charlotte too hard about opening up, but other than that, there isn't as much to worry about as I thought. Mason hasn't really said anything earth shattering, but I still feel a bit better for some reason. It's kind of an anti-Micah effect.

* * *

The next morning I'm really feeling the effects of my late night chat, though not nearly as much as after the O-Chem paper fiasco.

After the first class of the day, I see a text from Mara.

Where are you?

I respond, not thinking much of it. A couple of minutes later I take a blow from behind. I whirl around, startled.

"There you are," says Mara.

I relax.

"Hey! Good to see you."

"Are you sure?" The hostility is back in her voice. It occurs to me that maybe it was not actually a playful hit.

"Huh?"

"Are you sure you don't wish it was Charlotte?"

"Charlotte's not the one who makes my heart pound," I say because it's true.

She blushes slightly at that and seems to be thrown off her rant momentarily. Then she regains her footing.

"Yeah, I bet your heart was pounding awfully hard last night when *you forgot to call me like you said you would.*"

"Shoot."

"Yeah, shoot is right."

"I don't have an excuse."

"No, you don't." It's probably not just about the phone call. It's also the fact that I bailed on her during Swing Dance Club to take care of someone she hates.

"How can I make it up to you?"

The shadow of a smile returns to her face.

"You'd better have an absolute haymaker of a date planned for today."

"You're never going to know what hit you."

"Well, all right then." She still has a grouchy look on her face, but it's brightened up a bit.

I breathe a sigh of relief. Now I just have to figure out what we're doing.

Chapter 21

There's something odd about riding a bus to a sit-down restaurant. It's not like I know anyone with a Porsche, though, and this is one of the few date ideas I can think of that is both snazzy enough to be a surprise but not wild in a way that would leave Mara regretting that she ever knew my name. Not that it's *that* fancy. I'm still on a college student's budget after all. I manage to find a dusty suit coat in the back of my closet, though, so hopefully that will be enough to make it impressive.

Mara looks genuinely excited to see me, which is a relief. I don't think I could take much more of her wrath. On top of that, she's absolutely slaying in a hot pink blouse and a floral pattern skirt. It strikes me as strange yet again that a human this magnificent actually wants to go on a date with me. A couple of people on the bus give us weird glances.

"Let them judge. We're having too much fun," says Mara.

She smiles when she sees the restaurant, and I breathe a sigh of relief. It's as high-end as I can afford, but I don't know her well enough to gauge what her expectations are.

"I used to come here all the time on my birthday," she says happily.

I'm starting to get a little more comfortable around Mara, although I do still feel a little out of place. The conversation flows smoothly enough throughout dinner without too many awkward silences, but I find myself missing the snappy repartee that always seems to ooze from the cosmos between myself and Charlotte. It's a strange sensation. Mara's one of the most beautiful humans to exist, and she's still very much the one I'm crushing on. But my desire to help Charlotte has more *depth* to it somehow. It's like eating a hearty, healthy meal instead of downing an energy drink.

"Why don't you have a car?" Mara asks most of the way through our date.

I'm a lot more self-conscious about that question coming from her than from most people. Maybe it's because she seems to care about appearances to some degree. She would have been offended if I'd taken her to a fast food place tonight, for instance, whereas Charlotte would have made a snarky comment about it and then carried on with life. Ah! There I go thinking about Charlotte again. Focus!

"My dad doesn't want to pay for the insurance."

"Not even for a clunker?"

"He gets mad when I buy condiments at the grocery store."

"So then..." she glances down at the rib-eye in front of her.

"Birthday money from my grandma."

"And you spent it on me?" she says with a certain softness.

"I've been botching things so badly lately. I really didn't want to disappoint you again."

She looks down at her steak.

"You don't disappoint me, Levi."

"I--don't?"

"I know I can be clingy sometimes. You've slipped up a few times, but I know you mean well. It's just--I've been burned before, and it scares me."

"I'm probably going to slip up again at some point too," I say, thinking about future Swing Dance Club meetings. Or what if Charlotte calls me while I'm on a date again? I glance surreptitiously at my phone.

"You probably will. And I'll probably still get mad. But please don't see it as a failure. If I didn't want you," she places her hand over mine, "I wouldn't be here."

"Even though I don't own a car?"

"One day you're going to be a successful doctor with millions to your name and be driving more Mercedes than you know what to do with. It's really just as well. If you got the same type of car as anyone else now, you'd never find it in a parking lot."

"Yeah," I say. "I'd have to buy one of those fancy keychains to hang on the rearview--" I stop.

"What?"

Something has just clicked.

"Never mind." I try to bring myself back into the conversation, but it's a lost cause.

"Are you okay? You're zoning out on me," questions Mara.

"Yeah...sorry."

"Did I do something wrong?"

"No, it isn't that."

"You sure? It looks like something is bothering you."

"It's not about you, don't worry."

"Okay..."

I take another couple of stabs at engaging dialogue, but it's like wading through tar right now for some reason.

"Can I get a to-go box?" Mara asks the waiter.

"You want to go already?"

"No, but you do."

I shrivel up inside at that. There I go giving Mara reasons to be mad at me seconds after we've both committed to try harder.

"It's fine, we can go," she says, making me feel even worse.

I try again to talk to her during the walk back to the bus stop and on the ride home, but I feel like I have a sloth for a tongue, and everything I try feels dull and hollow.

"Look," she says finally, and I brace myself for more anger.

"I'm sorry I brought up the car thing. I know money is a touchy subject for you."

That's what she thinks this is about? Well, better than having her guess the real reason, given how she feels about Charlotte.

"You're good. I'm sorry for boring you with my financial woes."

"Levi, nothing about you is boring."

I'm suddenly acutely conscious of the fact that we're the only ones on the bus. I glance at the bus driver, who is too far away to hear us over the roar of the engine. Mara follows my gaze.

"Getting self-conscious, are we?"

She cups my face in her hands, which immediately makes me think of when I did that to Charlotte just yesterday, albeit for a completely different reason. The memory makes me feel squeamish, and I pull back ever so slightly, just enough to make Mara hesitate. I want to apologize, but it's one of those situations where actions speak louder than words. Just like yesterday, my hesitation has caused pain to someone I care about.

"Sorry," she says quietly and takes her hands back. She remains silent the rest of the way home. I *have* to stop making these mistakes. One of these days I'm going to make one that I can't fix.

Dropping her off on her doorstep is awkward.

"Thanks for the date," Mara says.

"Yeah. It was good."

"Talk to you tomorrow?"

"Yeah."

I don't know what kind of send-off she's expecting, and I don't want to do the wrong thing, so I end up settling for a quick side hug. I appreciate the effort she's putting into not getting angry at me, but right now it's making it difficult to know how to approach her.

As the door clicks shut behind her, my shoulders droop in exhaustion. I'm not done for the night, though, because I still have another stop to make before I'm done. Thanks to my date with Mara, I've finally figured out what Ajay is looking for.

Charlotte's apartment complex looks somehow more ominous than usual tonight. There are only a couple of windows alight in whole building. As soon as I arrive, it dawns on me that I should have called her first. Oh well. Hopefully she's here. A certain deep exhaustion that goes far beyond lack of sleep creeps up my back as I stand at the doorstep. I shrug it off and knock.

The door opens almost instantly and my heart leaps only to see—Grouchy Girl.

"Charlotte here?"

"Not for you."

"What's it to you?" I say, a bit irked that she's taking it upon herself to make my day more difficult.

She shrugs, not even humoring me with an answer.

Normally I would have just quit there, but this is important.

"Look, just tell her Levi is here if you don't believe me."

"Sure."

"Come on, woman, what did I ever do to you?"

She moves to slam the door shut, but I hold it open with a hand.

"Just tell her I'm here, please."

"She's not here."

"Bull."

She tries to slam the door again, but now there's a sound coming from inside, and she turns to look at it. There's a muffled voice. It's the groggy mumble of someone who's just woken up.

"Who is it?"

It's Charlotte. I push the door open farther.

"It's me."

"Levi!"

Grouchy Girl looks from me to Charlotte and back again, then presumably decides that it's not worth the effort and disappears back into the darkness. There's a bit of hoarseness to Charlotte's voice, like she's coming down with a cold.

"Are you getting sick?"

"No."

I eye her suspiciously, but there are more important fish to fry at the moment.

"Charlotte, you have to take the panda key chain out of your car."

Evidently this wasn't what she was expecting to hear, so she blinks slowly, gradually coming back to the land of the living from dreamland.

"What, why?"

"The person who's creeping on you has been trying to find it."

She nods softly, then seems to realize what I just said.

"No! I can't do that!"

"Why not?"

"I just can't."

That was not the response I was expecting.

"We need to move your car, then. He's been scouring parking lots for it, and if he finds it, he's going to know exactly where you live."

Charlotte takes a moment more to process this.

"Wait, how do you know that?"

"I had a—uh—run-in with him a while back."

She narrows her eyes suspiciously but evidently decides not to question me further.

"Okay."

She disappears back inside in search of her keys. My heart rate drops a little. If Ajay can't find her car or, even better, finds it in a place Charlotte doesn't actually live, maybe he will give up. Charlotte reappears again, and we head for her car. She's awfully calm for a woman who just found out that her stalker has been closing in. It's interesting how some situations she handles so well while others turn her inside out at the drop of a hat. She's cooperating, though, so I'm not going to complain.

"So where shall we move it?" I ask as I slide into the passenger seat.

"I don't want to leave it somewhere where it's going to get towed."

I nod.

"That rules out most places. Maybe we can park it in some random neighborhood…"

"And then I'll get the cops called on me for having a suspicious vehicle lurking around, and I'll have to camp out in your living room for a week."

"Don't say that like it'd be the end of the world."

"It's not the end of the world. At least it's not Siberia."

Her talking about my apartment gives me an idea.

"Hey, I think I still have the parking permit sticker they gave me when I moved in. You can just park by where I live."

"Sure. That'll give me an excuse to bug you."

"As long as you're willing to suffer through near-Siberian conditions."

"I'll survive."

The crisis is averted for the moment. It's a good thing Charlotte happened to be home.

"Why were you just sitting there by yourself on a Friday night? Don't you have a party to go to, or something?"

"I don't party."

"You don't?"

"No."

She provides no further explanation.

"Glad I could be your weekend entertainment, then."

"Can I get a refund?"

"I'll have to talk to my manager about that."

We arrive, and I run inside to find my parking sticker. It might be in that pile of stuff that's been shoved to the corner of my desk since the beginning of the semester.

"What are you looking for?" asks Micah, poking his head through my open door.

"Parking permit."

"You got a car?"

"Kind of. Not really."

"I've got an extra sticker if you want one."

"Thanks!" He disappears for a few seconds and tosses it onto my desk.

"Tell your girlfriend I said hi."

"She's not—never mind. Thanks again!"

I sprint back outside. Now I can just slap this bad boy on Charlotte's car, walk her back home...My thought process is interrupted by a resounding thud, loud enough to echo throughout the parking lot.

Charlotte's leaning against the hood of her car having an animated conversation with Mara, who is still dressed up from our date. She's up in her face, hand braced against the car window next to her. The sound I heard likely came from her hand thumping against the glass. The alarm bells start ringing. If Mara finds out I came here with Charlotte less than an hour after dropping her off, fireworks of a very different variety from those I experienced with her at the park would be an absolute certainty. Any sort of explanation about her stalker issues isn't going to land, especially given how distracted I was at the end of our date.

Fortunately, both women are so engaged in their conversation that they don't notice me standing there, which gives me a little more time to figure out the best approach. Then Mara raises her voice slightly, and now I can make out what she's saying.

"I don't expect you to pay me back. Just stay the (expletive) out of my life. And stay the (expletive) away from Levi."

It's only the second time I've heard her swear. Though now that I think about it, the other time was just yesterday and also directed at Charlotte. Charlotte says nothing. Her hands are dangling uselessly at her side. She doesn't seem in danger of a panic attack this time, but she's obviously still struggling. Suddenly Mara takes a step toward her and slaps her, a clean hit upside the head. Her head snaps back so hard it hits the car window behind her.

All the fear and confusion that has been building up inside of me evaporates like dew before the sun. I surge forward.

"Mara!" Her eyes widen as she looks up at me. "I get that you're jealous, but that is going too far!"

Her face hardens.

"You don't know what you're talking about, Levi."

"I know enough to get that you need to *back off*. If you don't like her, fine, but violence is uncalled for.

Especially about a conflict from the past that is better left dead and buried."

The irony of me arguing against digging into Charlotte's past after having spent the semester trying to do just that does not escape me. Somehow I don't think Mara's goal is reconciliation, though. Her face sharpens to a dangerous point.

"You have no idea how much I'm holding back right now. I'm going to be the bigger person here and not spell out every detail, but you'd better believe it's every bit as bad as I'm making it sound. Stay away from her, Levi. She isn't who you think she is."

"You've said that." I look over at Charlotte to make sure she's okay. Again, no panic attack, but I can tell from a single glance that she's emotionally shattered. Tears speckle her face.

"I don't care what she's done. I'm not abandoning her."

"You're a good guy, Levi," says Mara, turning to go. "But you can be real naive sometimes."

In the sky above us, rain begins to fall.

Chapter 22

"What did you do?" Charlotte asks accusingly. She gives me a shove. I sidestep it and hit the button to change the Walk signal across the street.

"What do you mean?"

"What do you mean what do I mean? Why did they turn my gas on?"

"I don't know why you assume I had something to do with it."

The light changes, and I step onto the crosswalk. Charlotte chases after me.

"Come on, out with it."

"Maybe your long-lost aunt took care of it for you or something."

She shoves me again. It's fairly gentle as shoves go, but it's hard enough to get the message across. I knew that some version of this was coming, but I wasn't expecting her to be so confident that I was the one behind it.

"If you already know what I did, I don't know why you're asking me about it."

"Why did you do it, Levi? I know you don't have that much more money than I do."

We reach the next section of sidewalk and continue around the corner.

"No, never mind. I know why. How did you pay for it? That's what I want to know."

"Why do you care?"

"I want to make sure you didn't sell your soul or something."

"Why? Were you in the market?"

"Shut up."

"Look," I tell her more seriously. "I know you told me you don't take handouts, but I'm not going to let you freeze. It's awfully difficult to succeed at being a singer when you have hypothermia."

At this, her resistance fades, as I knew it would. This was calculated, actually. Music rules a totally separate kingdom in her mind. Different rules apply there.

The dynamic between Charlotte and me has gotten interesting. We still walk back to her apartment every day even though we both know full well that her car is operational again. We've also started hanging out more like we used to.

As she relaxes more around me, she starts to show me parts of her personality that she hadn't let out before. Her almost childish love for stuffed animals, for instance. She doesn't actually own any, of course, being a broke college student who would get teased mercilessly if she did (including by me). One day on our way home, we pass a child in a stroller clutching a stuffed beaver, and she goes on and on about it. It makes me smile.

"It's just so *cute*," she swoons as we go by.

"How are you this excited about everything?"

Her glow fades a half-notch.

"Shouldn't I be?"

"Yes, you should."

She looks at me inquiringly. I take a deep breath and ask the question I'm really burning to know.

"What's music to you?"

She cocks her head.

"Where did that come from?"

I know how out-of-nowhere the question seems, but in reality it's been a long time coming.

"What's music to you?" I ask again. This time she senses, if not the reason for the question, at least the sincerity behind it.

"It is," she says slowly, "life. It's the one thing that's different. Everything around me is dull, dry, and meaningless. Everything hurts me or embarrasses me or kicks me to the curb. Everything except that. It runs through my veins, not because I inherited it, but because it's a part of me. It's *important.*"

"Why? What about it is important?"

This isn't me doubting her. I really want to understand.

"I don't know. I know it doesn't make any sense, but I can *feel* it. Like if I do my part well and let the magic out, it will fill the world with light. When I'm singing, I can feel that light rushing through me, pouring out to embrace everyone that it touches. There's something about it that's sacred, which is why I don't talk about it much."

Light. That was the word I myself used to describe what I saw in Charlotte in the library. In some ways her explanation isn't one at all, and yet there's something about the feeling behind it that helps me catch the briefest glimpse of what she's talking about. A memory flickers by, but it's too fast for me to catch it.

"You are," I say, "the most incredible person I've ever met."

She stops in the middle of the sidewalk.

"You mean that, don't you?"

I find that I do. It's not just one of those platitudes people throw around to make each other feel good.

"You'd better make it as a singer," I tell her. "You're right. The world needs your light. *I* need it. So that I can believe that life is more than all this dark gray mush."

"Yeah," she says. "There is a lot of mush. That's why this thing that's not is so special to me."

"I hope I can come to love something as much as you do one day."

She smiles a real smile.

"You sure you don't already?"

* * *

Between Charlotte and Mara, it's a minor miracle that I'm able to stay on top of my homework. Because yeah, I've been spending a lot of time with Mara as well. We've gone on a date every weekend since I moved Charlotte's car. They've gone decently well, and I've started to feel more comfortable around her, but it's still an endorphin overload just to be with her. I just can't get over the fact that someone as gorgeous as her is willing to give me the time of day.

Mara says she won't tell me the specifics of her beef with Charlotte. Oddly, this is what gets me over the slapping incident. For all her talk of people lying in the beds they make, the fact that she's refraining from giving me the whole story tells me that she *does* in fact want to leave the past buried. She says that she doesn't think that anything good would come from her gossiping about it, and I think I agree. At the same time, I do watch her anger a little more closely.

School has actually decreased in intensity lately as part of the calm before the storm leading up to finals. It's nice, and my grades outside of O-Chem are in a good spot, but it's hard to relax completely because none of them are so secure that a bombed final couldn't nuke my med school chances once and for all.

The lull ends up being quite important, though, as what follows after will wind up shaking me to my very core. The balls I've had to juggle so far this semester will feel like a cakewalk compared to what's coming next.

Chapter 23

So something cool happened

The fact that Charlotte's bothering to text me about it now rather than waiting until our walk back this evening is a big deal. She wouldn't do that unless it was important.

Yeah? What is it?

I won the audition to
sing the national anthem
at the volleyball game
today!

Right on!

She's finally breaking through! My heart soars. I check my schedule. Miraculously, it won't be hard for me to make it.

I'll be there.

She responds with a heart emoji followed by three firecrackers. Her excitement is so palpable, even over text, that it makes me smile in spite of myself.

"What's so funny over there?" asks Raymond. I quickly stow my phone away.

"Sorry. I got distracted for a second."

"Well undistract yourself then."

After what seems like an eternity, the Organic Chemistry assignment is nearing its completion. I haven't missed any more group meetings. Today we're actually meeting at my apartment, which I suggested as my way of making a peace offering. It seems to have worked to some extent; while Raymond is still chillier towards me than he was at the beginning, he's started smiling occasionally again.

So much has happened since we started the project that it feels like it was another lifetime ago. Back then the only thing on my mind was making it into medical school and not making a fool of myself with Mara. Come to think of it, both of those things are still relevant now. They've just been joined by a myriad of other things as well.

After I left the fateful group meeting a couple of weeks ago, my group scrambled to finish the paper and got it into a somewhat presentable state. Raymond wanted to talk to the teacher about flunking me, but Lindsay managed to convince him otherwise, pointing out that I technically still contributed more to it than he did. We ended up getting a B+. That's not a horrible grade, all things considered, but low enough to really crank up the pressure on our presentation. We've finished the slideshow and practiced it several times. Now we're putting some finishing touches on it.

"We can do this, guys," says Lindsay, trying to pump us up. "We do presentation assignments all the time. We've got this."

There's something different about this one, though, and we all know it. Nothing short of utter perfection is going to get us an A here.

"As long as we stick with the rubric and don't stand out too much for the wrong reasons, we should be fine," says Raymond.

We make a few more adjustments and call it a day. For all the positive talk, there's something about Organic Chemistry that makes you feel inevitable doom no matter how prepared you are.

After our group meeting, I head over to the volleyball arena for Charlotte's performance. I'm on pins and needles. Is it possible for me to feel more nervous than the person actually performing? She admitted recently under duress that the reason her voice went hoarse a little while ago was from vocal fatigue, which comes from practicing too much. I'm hoping that she's bounced back from it enough that she can put on a show she can be proud of.

I settle into my seat. I've gotten here extremely early, so I'll have time to pump her up a bit before the audience arrives. Just then Charlotte herself appears from the back somewhere and races up the bleachers toward me. She's smiling broadly, which makes for a nice change.

"Look who decided to show up."

"Don't sound so surprised. You know I wouldn't miss this for the world."

"Yeah. I know."

Charlotte tries to come up with a sassy comeback, but she's much too excited to find one.

"I still can't believe they're letting me do this."

"I can."

She swats the side of my head playfully.

"Shut up."

"Knock 'em dead."

Her eyes glow with pure happiness as she heads down to her courtside seat. I get now what she meant by using music to fill the world with light. Just being around her energy is infectious today. She's the most courageous person I know.

The teams explode onto the court to raucous applause and begin warming up. I sit back in my seat. The glow I've already been feeling grows even brighter.

The froth of life sloshes around me, sending endless ripples over my consciousness. Slowly the arena fills. Down on the playing floor both teams are beginning their warm-ups. One of the star players for the other team is arguing with her coach. The student section is emptier than it was earlier in the season when hopes of making it into the tournament had not yet been shattered, but we're still left with a healthy-sized crowd and enough noise to make my hair stand on end.

The arguing player stomps off the court, obviously enraged. Suddenly the memory that came up the other day when I was talking to Charlotte flashes by again, still too quickly for me to catch it. My mood drops slightly.

I refocus on Charlotte, who practically has lightning shooting out of her as she sits on the edge of her seat, waiting in rapt anticipation. There's no room for such dark thoughts on a day like today. After all, this will be the first time I've heard her sing. There's part of me that thinks that hearing her in her element will crack the last part of the code that will tell me what life is good for.

The announcer comes on over the loudspeaker:

"Ladies and gentlemen! Are you ready TO CHEER ON YOUR MAMMOTHS!"

The audience goes wild as the mascot, dressed in a mammoth costume, cartwheels onto the court, hurling free T-shirts into the crowd. Charlotte is looking a little more nervous now, but that's only to be expected. The angry volleyball player emerges from the locker room, hopefully much calmer, and takes her seat. It's game time.

Charlotte stands and gets into position on a bench just off stage as the announcer introduces the players by name. He rattles off the names of the opposing players politely, and they head to their end of the court half a stone's throw away from where Charlotte sits clutching her microphone.

The lights dim, and the building throbs with music as the home team runs in one at a time. Suddenly the player who had been arguing before leaps to her feet and begins screaming at her coach, but the music is so loud at this point that it's lost in the cacophony. I hope that they're able to sort out their differences before it's time for Charlotte to perform. The announcer reads off the next couple of names.

I glance back over at Charlotte, but something's off. She's hunched over, holding her head in her hands. At first it seems like the nerves have gotten to her, but there's something about her slumped posture that feels *wrong* somehow. She's too still, too rigid. Then the screaming player leaps forward, pointing emphatically at the sideline, and what's happening is suddenly obvious. I can't hear the yelling from way up here in the bleachers, but Charlotte can, and it's bringing on a panic attack at the worst possible time. The color drains from my face. There's no way I can help her from here. If I were next to her, I might be able to calm her down in time. As it is, I'm trapped up in the bleachers, light years away. Even at this distance I can see her start to shake.

"And .... MIIIIIIIIIIIIINA SIIIIIIIINGH!" Our team's ace makes a show of circling the court, waving her arms in an upward motion, egging on the crowd. As I watch, the microphone slips through Charlotte's fingers and rolls beneath her chair. *HELP HER!!* My heart cries out louder than the roar of the audience. I stand. Charlotte takes a deep breath, and for a second I think she's going to pull out of it, but then the player begins yelling again, and she stiffens, pulling her legs into her. I've *got* to be there.

My legs begin to move almost on their own. I don't know what I expect to be able to do. There's no way they're going to let me onto the court right now. For some reason that doesn't matter, though. To me, the path forward is as obvious as a lit up runway.

How many times in my life have I let what I was supposed to do get in the way of what I cared about? How many times have I believed something was impossible just because I couldn't see every step from start to destination?

No more.

I descend the stairs as quickly as I can without drawing attention to myself.

No more will I let my mind cheat my heart of what it knows to be true. No more will I let doubt and fear be my king. No more will I let my own interests stop me from being the blade at Charlotte's side. I want her to succeed more than I want breath.

I reach the bottom of the bleachers. Everyone is so focused on the players' complex nine-way handshake that they don't even notice me swing my legs over the edge and drop half a foot onto the court.

It's time for me to choose my path and own it, to let go of the subtle inhibitions that have subconsciously muddied the water my whole life. It's time to follow Charlotte's example and unleash my inner light.

I'm sprinting now, not caring who sees me, banking on the darkness and sheer amount of movement on the court and in the building in general to pull attention away from me. There's some security personnel around, but they're focused on the players right now, not the sidelines. I have mere seconds. There's no way she's going to be able to perform like this even if I make it there. This is going to be a catastrophe regardless of what I do. It doesn't matter. *She* is what matters, and I'm not going to let anything get in my way.

I. Love. Her.

Then I'm there. I'm by her side, the place that seemed literally hopeless to reach just seconds ago. I touch her gently on the shoulder and she looks up at me, air shooting in and out of her lungs rapid fire.

"Charlotte. Listen to the sound of my voice, Charlotte. I'm here. You're here. Just look at me." I hold my hands out to her. Slowly, she takes them. Somewhere in another lifetime I can hear the announcer saying something about the national anthem. I'm too late. I already know that. I trace my thumbs over the knuckles of her hands, using the sensation to bring her back to reality.

Something clicks back together, and she collapses into me. I wrap my arms around her, careful to be as gentle as possible so that the contact won't be too jarring. Then all of the lights in the arena go off. For a split second I think a miracle has hit us and the power's gone out, but half an eyeblink later the light returns. It's just one light this time, a spotlight. It's focused on us.

A ripple of confusion echoes through the crowd as a moment that held only the two of us suddenly becomes the focal point of the entire building.

"No matter what happens, it's going to be okay," I whisper in her ear. I'm not going to let this be the reason she gives up. I *will not*. A spark catches in my heart and suddenly all of life is aglow with a pure, deep radiance. As she begins to relax, I hold her even tighter.

"Remember the light, Charlotte. Remember it. You said it was important."

She nods her head slowly.

"So give it to them." I reach underneath the seat for her microphone and offer it toward her.

"Give them the light."

In breath. Out breath.

She reaches forward and takes the microphone.

"Oh saaaay can you seeee, by the dawn's early liiiight,"

It's the same song I've heard a hundred thousand times, but this one is different. My mind tells me it's because I know the stakes, because I know how much it means to Charlotte. My heart disagrees. As the undulating melody echoes across the otherwise silent auditorium, it seems to carry with it her very soul. The notes pierce my being, setting it aflame. I look into her violet eyes and see eternity. For a moment the surface of life itself is peeled back, revealing the silent, unutterable secrets beneath.

The song ends. The final bar ripples across space and time, fading slowly into nothingness. For a moment there is silence.

Then a deafening cheer goes up from the crowd. The spotlight goes out, but Charlotte stays there a second longer. I realize suddenly that I'm still standing right next to her, having been in full view of the spotlight the whole time. I hope I didn't take away from her performance.

"Thank you," she whispers. The lights turn back on and the volleyball game begins.

"Of course. Let's get out of here."

No one seems to notice as we head for the exit. Charlotte goes to hand off the microphone. The stage hand in charge of such things, a brunette in her twenties, takes it from her.

"Pretty decent singing out there. You can really belt it out. Have you ever thought of taking lessons?"

That rubs me the wrong way. What Charlotte does is not just "pretty decent singing." It feels disrespectful for her to treat it so mundanely. Getting mad about it won't accomplish anything, though, so I bite my tongue.

The wind outside is bitterly cold, but I hardly even feel it. We wander off, going nowhere in particular.

"Is that always what it's like?" I ask finally.

She shakes her head.

"Not always. The best times, yes."

"What the stage hand said. That's why you're so careful about telling people about it."

"Yeah."

She seems to have something on her mind, but I don't ask because if she really wants to share, she's going to come out with it on her own. Suddenly she pulls into me so hard that it forces me to come to a full stop. She looks up at me, the twin violet gems on her face blazing into mine.

"I like you, Levi."

I can see her immediately regret saying it. Her eyes are full of fear. My lips part, seeking the precise way to put it. Charlotte pulls away from me, bracing herself.

"It's not that I don't like you. Actually I kind of love you."

She peeks out at me.

"Kind of?"

"It's complicated."

"I've got all day."

"I haven't ever really thought of you romantically. I mean, you're not ugly or anything."

Charlotte gives me a death glare.

"It's just that I've been so determined to help you reach your dreams that there hasn't really been room for anything else."

"But..?"

"But when we were in there just now, I realized that my determination to help you become a singer *is* love. It was just so unassuming that I didn't see it for what it is."

Somehow the awe I feel when I see Charlotte sink her teeth into that elusive part of life I'm always grasping for and my constant, quiet drive to help her be her best self has blossomed into the very thing I was sure that it wasn't.

"So, what? You love me *platonically* or something?"

"Kind of."

"You're just the king of clarity today, aren't you?"

"Look, I don't know, okay? I just want you to be happy, I guess. I want it really, really bad."

"I know."

Suddenly it hits me why she was so confident that I was behind turning her heat back on.

Charlotte's eyes are locked on my mouth. She's slowly moving towards me, her own lips parting, as if hoping to bind me firmly to her with a kiss so that I can't escape out of her grasp. I put a hand on her shoulder to stop her.

"Charlotte, you know that I'm kind-of-sort-of dating Mara, right?"

As she starts to wilt, I quickly add:

"But I'm not really even sure that I want to."

"What do you want?"

"I don't know. You wanted clarity, there it is: I don't know what I want."

She takes a half step back, not sure whether to pull away.

"So what does that mean for us?"

"You know I'm not going to abandon you."

"Yeah. I know."

"I'm going to do what I've always done. I'll be there when you need me. I'll help you overcome your panic attacks and find a way for you to share your talent with the world."

"I don't know if that's possible."

"Of course you don't. That's what makes it a leap of faith."

She lets out a breath, neither relieved nor broken.

"I guess that's enough for now."

We make it back to Charlotte's apartment without incident. Gloomy Girl is there, which normally would have bothered me, but today it doesn't seem to matter.

"Is she drunk?" She asks me.

"No."

"Okay." She disappears into her room.

Charlotte collapses onto the couch. In a matter of minutes she falls asleep. I let out a breath that I've been holding for the past two hours. I stand there a moment, just watching her.

How did she do it? How did she push through a literal panic attack to sing tonight? Is she an angel, or something?

It strikes me that if I spent my entire life trying to help people reach their potential only to succeed in one single solitary instance, I would be okay with that. If, that is, Charlotte was the one it worked for.

Maybe I do know what I want.

The stars have a luster I've never seen in them before as I make my way home from Charlotte's apartment. The trees, the sky, the asphalt, the universe, have *never* been the way they are now. It's like someone has sprinkled fairy dust over everything, endowing it with a certain crispness I've always longed for but have never been able to put into words, not even now. It's a moment that I'll remember for the rest of my life. That's partially because it's a moment I'll frequently cling to in order to prove to myself that what I'm fighting for is real, that life is actually more than the sum of its parts. It's

also partially because it's after this night under the stars
that everything begins to fall apart.

Chapter 24

The next day I drive Charlotte to school. We don't coordinate beforehand. She just shows up in the morning with the keys in her hand, and I take them. We spend our class breaks studying side by side in the library and eat lunch on the grassy area outside of the Fine Arts Building. At first it's just nice to have her around so much. But soon I realize that something is horribly wrong.

It starts when I have to leave for my class that starts at one. I catch this look in her eye of pure terror as I'm packing up to leave.

"You okay?"

"I don't know."

She tries to shake it off, but it's clear she's getting rocked by something. She's not trying to downplay it the way she used to, but whatever's wrong seems to be something that's hard to put into words.

"Do you need me to cut class to stay with you?"

"No," says her mouth as her eyes say yes.

Her relief is palpable when I sit back down again. I tell myself it's a one-time thing. I tell myself her panic attack yesterday must have taken more out of her than I realized. Part of me knows that I'm lying.

An hour later when it's time for her own class, she's still sitting there, looking nervously up at the clock. I grab her by the shoulders so she won't be able to escape.

"What's going on?" I ask her.

She shrinks beneath my gaze

"I had a panic attack last night," she manages finally.

"I know. I was there."

"Not that one. Another one."

"You had two on the same day?"

A flood of guilt washes over her like she's done something horrible. I grab her hand, suddenly afraid that she's going to have yet another one as she's sitting there.

"What happened?"

Charlotte doesn't want to say it, but she knows that she has to. She grits her teeth and forces the words out.

"I woke up in the middle of the night, and you weren't there."

"Isn't that true most nights?"

"The worst part of panic attacks," she says finally, "Is the *fear* of panic attacks."

"Right. You've said something like that before."

"In the past I've only ever gotten panic attacks when I'm out in public. I think that's because when I'm home, I feel safer."

I nod.

"Well, last night, I had a nightmare about something that happened a long time ago. It was probably because of all the stress from yesterday. Anyway, I woke up anxious from that, and then I looked over and you weren't there--"

I'm starting to get the picture now.

"You were already keyed up from everything that went on yesterday, and then the fear of being alone pushed you over the edge, even though you were in the safety of your apartment."

"Yeah."

"So today you're extra sensitive to being left alone."

"Yeah."

I do a quick calculation. If I do some extra credit, I can probably get by without the attendance points from my next class.

"Look, obviously this can't be an every day thing, but I can probably ditch the rest of my classes for today, if you want."

There's the guilt again. She doesn't want to be a burden, but the weight that she's carrying at the moment is just too much to turn me down.

"I guess I can stand you a little longer."

I settle in for the long haul.

Charlotte, as expected, sticks to me like absolute superglue. To be perfectly honest, there's a guilty little corner of me that likes being latched onto this tightly, especially by someone as special as she is. Having spent most of my life feeling like no one would notice if I suddenly vanished from off the face of the earth, being clung to with a vice grip makes for a nice change. That said, I'm still worried. What if Charlotte isn't feeling better tomorrow? Am I supposed to drop out of school just to make sure she doesn't have another panic attack?

A couple of hours into the afternoon I get a call from my dad. Normally I wouldn't answer it with anyone else around, but today I don't have much of a choice.

"Hello?"

"Why is there a $639 charge on your account?"

I glance nervously over at Charlotte, who is poking through a math assignment. Of all the awful timing for him to find out. I talk as quietly as possible in hopes that she won't notice what I'm saying.

"I met this girl who was going through a hard time, and--"

"Are you kidding me?"

I flinch. I knew this was coming, but even I wasn't expecting this much wrath.

"Are you kidding me?" he says again. "A girl? I didn't work sixty hours a week for ten years just for you to give my money to charity!"

"She needed it, Dad."

"You are not to use that money on your girlfriend!"

"She isn't my girlfriend. And it was a one-time thing. If I cut my food budget next semester I should still be okay."

"You'd better be, or you can forget about going to graduate school."

He hangs up. I let out a breath. That one hurt.

"Levi." It's Charlotte. She's got that concerned look on her face again.

"Did you spend your tuition money on our gas bill?"

Drat. She overheard. I know I can't lie to her, especially since I've been trying to get her to be honest with me.

"I'm not going to let you freeze, Charlotte."

"I told you I was going to drag you down."

She scoots closer and lays her head on my shoulder.

"And now you're stuck with me."

I can see the conflict roiling inside of her. Guilt that I've done all this on her account. Fear of being alone. Sadness from the conversation she just heard. How does she do it? How does she survive having all that duking it out in her head at the same time?

"Your dad's a real dingbat."

"He's been poor his whole life. It makes him possessive of the money he does have.

"Well, he could use a chill pill."

"Yeah. He is my dad, though."

The afternoon limps on. We finish our homework and wander around campus. We both just want to clear our heads. We both find it rather difficult. The chill of the air seems to seep into our very souls.

"We were doing just fine with the space heaters," she murmurs as we make our way through the orchestra room.

"I know."

"You shouldn't have done it without asking me."

"I know."

It feels like this day will never end.

"Anything else you want to do on campus?"

She shakes her head. We go to the car.

Back at my apartment complex, I hop out and try to hand the keys back, but she doesn't take them.

"Can I come in?"

I picture another confrontation with Micah with nowhere to run, but I'm not going to let that stop me today. It's time to stop letting my fear of him hold me back.

"Sure."

The living room's empty. I breathe a sigh of relief. I'd deal with Micah if I had to, but this will be much easier without him breathing down my neck. We go in and set up camp on the sofa. Charlotte lays her head on my shoulder. I wonder if I should stop her.

This isn't fair to Mara, I think as the rhythmic whoosh of Charlotte's breath against my neck lulls me into a catatonic state. Mara isn't technically my girlfriend, but she's close enough that I really can't keep doing this. There's a big part of me that wants to jettison the dating stuff entirely and just focus on helping Charlotte through her panic attacks. What has romance ever really done for me? Or anyone, for that matter? It seems to me that all it ever brings is selfishness.

I have to bite the bullet and just do it. There's no way to make it any easier than it's going to be. I look over at Charlotte, who looks close to falling asleep on me. The fact of the matter is that I want to help her. Nothing is more important to me than that, not even having a hot girlfriend.

The door explodes off its hinges.

Luckily I'm between it and Charlotte, so I bring my arm up defensively and try to shift her behind me as much as possible. We're being attacked! A figure rushes towards me, hand extended. I knock it out of the way reflexively.

"Why of all the--" says the intruder, and I suddenly realize who it is. Speak of the devil, it's Mara. Charlotte starts awake and, seeing who has just burst in, jerks away from me like she's been bitten by a snake. This unfortunately kills any fleeting hope I had of explaining this in a way that doesn't make me look like a dirty cheater.

"I'm so dumb," says Mara with unnerving calmness. "I bought every line you gave me, every excuse you made for how you were just helping her with her 'stalker issue.'" Her voice hardens. "And then you go and flaunt your girlfriend in front of the whole volleyball arena--"

Mara watches the volleyball games. The realization smacks me in the face with the force of a freight train. She saw everything. But surely it was clear that something was wrong and that I was stepping in to help her?

"Look, she was having a panic--"

"I'm not going to be gaslighted by that—that *thing*," she says, pointing at Charlotte.

A door opens down the hall. It's Micah, who apparently has been home all along, out to see what the commotion is all about. Oh, great.

I stand, positioning myself between Mara and Charlotte.

"If you could just list--"

"You're the one who isn't listening, Levi! If you had, maybe you wouldn't have picked a girlfriend who goes around mugging people in dark alleys."

Charlotte almost unconsciously pulls herself into a fetal position, as if trying to ward off the oncoming verbal assault.

"What?" I ask, confused.

"She jumped me, Levi!"

"She...jumped you?"

Mara nods.

"Five years ago. I was with my brother. He tried to pull out his phone to call the cops, and one of her *friends*," she twists the word like a knife, "stabbed him in the thigh. They got him so deep that it gave him permanent nerve damage."

Wait a minute. Didn't Mara say something once about becoming a nurse because of some kind of medical situation? Doesn't that mean--

"She ruined his baseball career and gave him a limp for the rest of his life, all because *she* couldn't go without her drug money."

Drug money? Charlotte is, unsurprisingly, starting to shake. I sit down again next to her and put my hand on her shoulder. To my surprise, that's enough for it to stop. I know Mara won't like it, but if I can head off this panic attack before it starts, it might help Charlotte regain her mental stability. Or at least prevent it from getting worse.

"Of *course* you side with--"

"That makes a lot of sense," I say quietly. "I get why you wouldn't be able to just forget that. You're right, I've been judging you too harshly."

That takes some of the steam out of her sails, but there's still plenty to go around.

"Then why are you sitting over there instead of with me?"

"I just want to help her. And I don't think I can give her what she needs right now and date you at the same time."

"What, you're suddenly in love with her or something?"

"Kind of."

"You're *kind of* in love with her? What does that even mean?"

"I don't know. I'm still trying to figure that out myself."

Mara's voice has a slight quiver to it.

"I looked the other way so many times when it came to Charlotte because I thought I could trust you. But at the end of the day, you're going to throw what we were building away because some random druggie has to live with the consequences of her actions?"

My insides are having a full-blown wrestling match. I hate this.

"I do care about all of that, Mara."

"He says as he's *in the arms of another woman!*"

There are tears in both her eyes and voice now. She's speaking louder now, not quite a shout, but clamorous enough for me to wish the walls were three feet thicker.

"Maybe it would be better to talk about this another time," says Micah, stepping forward. "Unless you want the apartment upstairs to call the cops on us."

Mara stops and bends over, sides heaving. She's not wrong. I *have* betrayed her, and for her worst enemy, no less.

"I'm sorry."

"I know," says Mara through her tears. "I know I should hate you, but I just can't."

Somehow that makes it even worse.

"The one I hate is that abomination of a human being sitting over there."

"She's not an abomination."

"And how would you know? Were you there when she jumped me? How many people out there are scared to walk down dark alleys because of what she did to them?"

"I know, but she's not an abomination."

"What would it take? What would it take, Levi, for you to see her true colors? If she murdered someone?"

I don't have an answer for that. My head is spinning.

"It's time to go," says Micah again.

Mara turns and walks to the door. At the threshold she stops and looks back at me.

"Don't let her ruin your life, Levi." With a click of the door behind her, she's gone.

Chapter 25

"Thanks for getting her to leave."

"No problem," says Micah.

"What? No snarky comment about how Nietzsche disapproves of my dating choices?" I probe.

"What do you think I am, a walking philosophy textbook?"

"...Aren't you?"

He doesn't answer that. I turn my attention to Charlotte, who is trembling again. I slowly place my hand on her shoulder. She doesn't shrink away, which is a good sign. I don't think she's in a full-blown panic attack, but there's still enough anxiety in the room for the both of us. After a minute or two, she's calm enough for a conversation.

"I don't think she's coming back anytime soon," I say, acutely conscious of the fact that Micah hasn't gone back into his room yet.

"Please don't leave me." It comes out as a whimper.

"I'm not going to leave you."

"I'm a really awful person, Levi."

"No you're not."

"I am."

I'm not sure what to say to that.

"Are you okay to walk home by yourself?"

"No."

"I'll come with you."

The crisp air outside seems to help ground her the rest of the way back into the present. It's helpful for me, too. That deep sense of exhaustion is back, likely due to the sheer amount of intensity I've been dealing with lately. I shake it off. I can rest when the crises are over.

"Tell me about the drugs," I say. To my surprise, she answers.

"I grew up around it. My biological parents, aunts, uncles, cousins, almost all of them used at some time or other. Some of them got sober for a while, but most of them fell back into it eventually. My parents would disappear all the time when they were high, and I never knew when they'd be back. I'd have to make my own food, get myself to school, all that."

"Just yourself? You're an only child?"

She nods.

"Sometimes one of my aunts would come over to check on me, but most of the time I was by myself."

"That's why you hate being alone so much."

"Yes."

"And then you started using drugs too?"

She nods again.

"I was twelve the first time I smoked something other than a cigarette. Then in middle school--"

"Hold up." I raise a hand. "*Twelve?*"

"Yeah," she answers, looking self-conscious.

"How does a twelve-year-old even get a hold of something like that?"

"Well, it was all around me, right? I was at a sleepover at one of my cousin's house and they gave me some. It wasn't like I used all the time at that age, though."

I'm aghast. This is a lifestyle so far beyond anything I'm familiar with that it's hard to even imagine. She goes on.

"Anyway, in middle school I started dabbling in some of the harder stuff. A school counselor got wind of the fact that my parents were disappearing for weeks on end, and child welfare stepped in."

"Wait, *weeks*?"

She looks uncomfortable again.

"It got worse when I was a little older. They took me away from my parents and put me into a group home. My parents got sober for a little while to try to get me back, but they ended up slipping up one too many times and had their parental rights taken away."

"And how did all of that lead to...mugging people?" There's no delicate way to put it.

"When I was fourteen, I ran away from the group home and lived on the streets. We used to jump people to get money for food. And drugs," she adds reluctantly. "Most of the time we'd take a few dollars from them and let them go but with—what was her name? Mara?"

"Yes."

"Like she said, her brother tried to call the cops and one of the—people I was with got scared and stabbed him. He was bleeding really badly so I called 911, and then when they picked him up, they got me too."

"You let yourself get caught to save him?"

"Don't make me sound like such a saint, Levi." There's a bit of a bite to her voice. "If we hadn't jumped them, none of that would have happened."

We're not even halfway back to Charlotte's place. I'm walking as slowly as possible, making sure I'm getting the whole story.

"Were you in a gang?"

She shook her head.

"I knew people who were in gangs, but I was never in one myself. We were just a bunch of kids trying to survive and get high as much as possible."

"How are you so..."

"Normal?"

"Yeah."

"A couple of reasons. My aunt who was married to my father's brother didn't use. She's the one who always checked in on me. She let me live with her for a few months at a time. I learned to sing from her, and she taught me a lot of the things my mother should have.

"Also, I was really only using drugs heavily for the few months I was on the streets. If I'd been using much longer than that, it would have been a lot harder for me to quit. It was possible to get drugs in the group home too, but they were pretty rough on us if we got caught, so I didn't use much then.

"After the...thing with Mara's brother, they sent me back in until I got a foster family. My placement adopted me a few months later, and I had a more normal childhood after that. I still used off and on for a little while, but one day I was looking in the mirror, and it hit me that I couldn't see myself in my reflection anymore. So I quit and started taking school seriously so I could get into college."

"You quit just like that?"

"It wasn't quite that straightforward. I slipped up a few times before I was completely sober. Also, the fact that I had singing to pour myself into helped a lot because it gave me something positive to focus on."

I thought about the way putting so much effort into Charlotte has been improving my own life. I guess having singing in her life had a similar effect on her in some ways. It makes sense now that she sees it as something sacred. It's been the only thing standing between her and insanity for a long time now.

"So when you got the band-aid for me from the nurse's station--"

"I picked the lock," she admits reluctantly.

"Well, it was for a good cause. It's not like you were robbing jewelry stores."

Then something else clicks.

"Is that why you don't go to parties? Because you're afraid of relapsing?"

She nods.

"The fact that my lifestyle is so different now is a huge part of me being able to maintain my sobriety. If I were to let that other world creep back into my life to any degree, there's a risk that I could fall back into drugs."

"Even now, so long after?"

"It's always something I'll have to look out for, Levi."

She falls silent. We're at the end of her story. She's been so engrossed in the telling of it, but now that she's done, the fear seeps back onto her face. I know her well enough by now to see that regardless of what she tells herself rationally, deep down she believes I'm going to turn and run now that I know the truth.

"Charlotte—"

She braces herself for the blow.

"I'm disappointed that you think that's enough to make me ditch you."

She looks up at me.

"Do you honestly think I'm such an awful friend that I'm going to kick you to the curb just because you've had a hard life?"

"But I lied to yo--"

"How is anything you've said to me a lie? You just kept some very personal things to yourself until you were ready to talk about it."

"I've been pretending to be something I'm not."

"Baloney. You think the drugs define you? You're someone who is chasing her dreams despite all odds. That's who you are *now*. How is that not more important than the mistakes you made in the past?"

"There's this..." she pauses, "hole inside of me. I've tried to cover it up in a hundred thousand different ways, but it never lasts for long. I try to shove it down and paste a smile on my face, and things will kind of hold together for a while, but then something like," she gestures vaguely into the air, "this thing with Mara happens, and it all falls apart all over again. I'm so sick of fighting."

She's not making eye contact with me. I suspect it makes it easier to get the words out.

"Then I'll fight with you," I tell her. "That's why I'm here."

"You don't really get it. If you did, you'd run screaming."

"Then I guess there's a lot of screaming in my future. And I'll be running toward you, not away."

This elicits a hint of a smile, and I feel like an absolute superhero.

"You're right," I continue. "I don't have any idea what it's like to live through what you've been through. But I do have something at least as valuable."

"What's that?" She's sounds genuinely confused.

"I know what it's like to live a normal life."

We reach her apartment. She looks over at me. She doesn't say anything, but I can tell she's trying to find an excuse to make me stay longer. I make it easy for her.

"Can I come in?"

Her relief is palpable as she opens the door.

"I probably shouldn't stay too long because you need to get some sleep," I say as soon as we're inside. As usual, we have the apartment to ourselves.

Now that I understand about the hole inside of her, a number of other things makes sense. Like how everything I say to try convince her that she isn't inconveniencing me seems to just bounce off of her. That doesn't mean I'm going to stop trying.

"Thank you," I tell her.

"For what?"

"For letting me in."

I don't mean opening the door to her apartment.

"For burdening you with my baggage?"

"For trusting me with something I'm sure you haven't told many other people."

"Stop it."

"What?"

"Feeding me that heart-melty stuff. I feel like I'm about the catch cooties."

She leans back against me. We stay like that for a while, just existing. Finally I check the time and pull away.

"Sleep, now."

"Yes, sergeant."

I stand at the door, trying to come up with the words to help her understand how grateful I am to her. Whatever they are, they don't exist in English. So I say the next best thing.

"See you around, Charlotte."

With that, I disappear into the night.

Chapter 26

The sting of losing Mara hits on the way home. I'd been shoving it down for Charlotte's sake, but now that there's room for it to surface, it's all I can think about. Even though it was the only thing to be done, I can't help but feel bothered by how thoroughly Mara got the short end of the stick.

There's no room for middle ground here. I either go all in on helping Charlotte, or I don't. Trying to live in both worlds at once doesn't work.

It doesn't make sense that Charlotte is afraid of me abandoning her. Right now I'm shocked that *she* wants to stick with *me*.

At home, Micah is waiting for me.

"Thanks again for smoothing things over," I tell him.

"No problem."

I glance over at my laptop, but there's no way any more homework is getting done tonight.

"You didn't take my advice about not meddling in things you don't understand," says Micah.

"I'm not Charlotte's therapist. I'm just helping her out for a while."

"In what world is making someone so dependent on you that they can't function on their own 'helping' them?"

It's probably because Micah's been so uncharacteristically helpful today that this feels like it comes out of left field.

"I wouldn't call it dependent."

"She's using you as a crutch! That girl came at her, and instead of allowing her to take care of her own problems, you stepped in and dealt with it for her. It's so patronizing. She can't even walk home by herself without you there. Does that sound like helping to you?"

I don't have a good answer for him.

"But her panic attacks--"

"--Are something that you can't overcome for her. Do you think so little of her that you don't believe she can find a way to work through her own issues?"

Aughhh! The way he twists my words! But there is some truth mixed in there this time. I *am* worried she'll want to cling to me again tomorrow. I don't know what the right balance is between being supportive and being a crutch. This is the point in the conversation when I normally offer some kind of defense which is then systematically dismantled. Today I just don't have it in me.

"You're right, I should just give up," I say with as much bitterness as I can muster and collapse headlong onto the couch.

Micah stands there with his mouth partly open, somewhat taken aback.

I take a step closer.

"Everything I touch turns to mush, so I should just stop and bury my head in the sand like the loser that I am."

"Being honest about harsh realities is unpleasant, but it's the only way to find the truth," Micah responds finally.

I say nothing, and eventually he goes back to his room. I feel completely defeated. All the positive feelings

I'd had only half an hour ago at Charlotte's apartment have evaporated like so much mildew being scoured in vinegar. Have I just been deluding myself? Maybe it would have been better to let Charlotte work through things on her own today.

Suddenly I realize that this sense of everything I do being a mistake is probably at least somewhat similar to what Charlotte feels every day. How does she survive like this? It makes me want to crawl into a deep dark hole and never return. It feels like every bright, happy thing that has happened since I met Charlotte was nothing but a mirage, a myth worthy of the *Squatch Watch*. Maybe I should disappear out of her life and let her find her own path to healing.

I let myself stay like that for about an hour. Finally I lurch to my feet. There's another day to be had tomorrow. No sense facing it on low sleep.

The next morning I'm a little standoffish when Charlotte comes over to go to campus with me. I don't want to do anything to make her feel rejected, but Micah's comments about her being too dependent on me are making me second-guess myself. So much for not letting fear take over. She can obviously sense it, because she soon comments:

"Pillow rub you the wrong way last night?"

"You could say that. Sorry, I'm a bit out of it."

I make a couple of half-hearten attempts at the normal banter, but it comes off as awfully flat.

It's not a particularly good day. There are plenty of things that don't go wrong, but my overall gloom magnifies the ones that do a hundred times over. Charlotte sticks to me like glue again. I let her because I don't know what else to do, but I do go to class like normal. I can tell she's disappointed by that, but she doesn't say anything. Somehow that only makes it worse. To top it off, it's a bit of a cloudy day, which casts a pall of actual physical darkness over the world to accent the shadows that are already in my mind.

"Have you ever been to the Comedy Club?" asks Charlotte.

The question is so unexpected that it completely breaks me out of my reverie. We're eating packed lunches at a picnic table in the courtyard of the humanities building. I've been quieter than normal, and she's picked up on it.

"No. Are you gunning to make your own singing stand-up show or something?"

She shrugs.

"Just thought it would be fun."

I glance over my schedule. I have my last O-Chem presentation run-through this afternoon and a short essay due tomorrow in a different class, but if I can hammer out a rough draft before my last class of the day, and since it seems to be important to her for some reason...

"Sure. Let's do it."

* * *

A little of the haze has lifted by the time I make my way to Lindsay's apartment for our last group meeting. That's a good thing, because I need all of my brainpower for making the final adjustments to our presentation.

"We need to add another practical application for E1 reactions," I note as I go through the rubric with a fine-toothed comb for the millionth time. "It says we need three, but we only have two so far."

"They use a lot of E1 reactions in pharmaceuticals," suggests Lindsay. "I bet we can get another one from there."

"I'll look it up," says Raymond.

"While you're doing that, let's practice your section again, Levi, and make sure you make good eye contact, or we'll lose a couple of points for that."

I give my part of the presentation again, being sure to lock eyes with Lindsay as I do so.

"A little too much that time, but better."

Raymond hands over what he found to Lindsay, and we go through the entire thing one more time. There's something about practicing so much that makes this feel like an even bigger deal. Not that it wasn't critically important to our grade in the class already, but the more I practice, the more my nervousness blossoms. I keep picturing my dad's face the moment he learns that we've completely bombed it. Knowing him, that would likely be enough for him to make me pay back the money he's spent on tuition with interest. I shudder. It's a good thing I soon won't have to deal with this project anymore.

*   *   *

Charlotte is waiting for me when I get back to campus. She hooks her arm around mine, grinning fiendishly. It makes me wonder what she's up to.

Comedy Club at this university is basically an open mic session where people from the club test out new material. These are first-time performers, so I'm not expecting too much, but having something to break me out of the sheer intensity of the last couple of days is nice. The first couple of sets are fairly average. I force a couple of chuckles to be supportive, but I'm not really feeling it. The next comic's piece is about goats that have too many laundry baskets. The one after that sounds like it could've been written by seven-year-olds.

Charlotte is doing her best not to cringe. I'm perusing the internet on my phone to find out if second-hand embarrassment can be fatal. The final acts are pure torture. The audience is so worn out, they're hardly even offering sympathy laughs by the end. The last guy keeps forgetting his lines and looks like a particularly juicy bison performing for a crowd of saber-tooths.

There's a collective sigh of relief as he brings the show to a haphazard close.

"If that's what the competition's like, you might have a future in comedy after all," I tell Charlotte on the way out.

She shakes her head.

"If I had any talent for it, I'd lose it just hanging around that bunch."

She looks a bit put out for some reason.

"What's wrong?" I ask.

"I hoped that would to cheer you up."

"Cheer me up?"

"You've been a giant cloud of boiled Brussels sprouts all day, and I just thought--"

"Boiled Brussel—hahaha!" I laugh harder than I did through the whole comedy show. "Wait, that was you trying to cheer me up?"

"Don't laugh!"

We're wandering aimlessly about campus. I love the feeling of the two of us being entirely alone in such a big place. I look over at Charlotte, really look at her. There's genuine disappointment in her eyes.

"I understand what you meant now," I say.

"Which part?"

"When you said that my mistakes were still the right thing, somehow."

"Yeah?" She brushes a golden lock of hair behind her ears.

"Do you know how long it's been since someone has cared that I had a bad day?" There's a hitch is my voice that surprises me. "Do you know how long I've been alone?"

"Do you know how many days I've spent surrounded by people, literally surrounded, on this campus without talking to a single soul? Do you know how many times I've tried to branch out only to be shut down? The only other person I can kind of call a friend besides you is a human dystopian novel, for crying out loud!"

Charlotte wipes a tear from my cheek with her thumb.

"I'm just saying you could have thrown me in a pit of alligators to cheer me up, and I'd still see it as the most wonderful thing you've ever done."

"You'd better watch what you say. I'm taking notes." She turns her head away, but I think I catch a glance of a tear of her own dribbling down her own chin. "We'd better head back."

I mean, if she's doing things like this for me, it probably means she isn't too dependent on me, right? I still feel unsettled and have a deep sense of having screwed everything up somehow, but even though it's nighttime now, my day still looks a little brighter.

Chapter 27

Today I'm preparing for battle. I do a final scan through my notes and load my flash drive with the presentation on it into my backpack like a gladiator polishing his sword and strapping on his shield before his last day on Earth.

There's a knock on the door, and I go to let Charlotte in.

"Knock 'em dead," she tells me.

"That's what I'm here for."

"No, you're here to drive me crazy."

"You'd better hang onto your sanity for as long as possible, then."

We walk to campus. Charlotte tries to hold my hand, but instead I push her playfully on the shoulder. She grumbles a bit, but with the feeling of someone who's going through their morning routine. Neither of us is entirely sure where exactly we stand with each other, just that it isn't quite a relationship. Whatever it is, it's something pretty special to us.

"Are you sure you're going to be okay by yourself for that long?"

She nods.

"I'm just going to hang out in the library for a while. It'll be fine. College textbooks aren't *that* scary."

I haven't cut class for her since that first day, but we still spend an awful lot of time with each other. I'm still trying to figure out if that's just what she needs right now, or if Micah was right and we should pare it back some.

"I'll swing by after I'm done."

"You'd better."

She gives me a hug for good luck, and I take my leave. It's quite early in the morning, but my adrenaline is high enough that I'm fully alert even without caffeine. I run through my part again in my mind for reassurance as I head toward the hard sciences building. I hope I don't miss anything on the rubric. The very thought makes me die a little inside.

It's the first day all semester that everyone is in the classroom not only on time, but *early*. The auditorium is pulsing with nervous energy. I find Lindsay and Raymond three-quarters of the way to the top and sit down next to them. Raymond proffers a polite nod. I run through my part again, not because I really need to, but mostly because I want something to distract myself from what I'll soon be doing in front of the class.

My phone buzzes, and I pull it out. It's Charlotte, wishing me good luck, no doubt. I open the message.

There's a weird guy staring at me

My adrenaline spikes for reasons entirely unrelated to chemistry. *It's probably just some guy who thinks she's cute.* There's a twinge of jealousy at the thought. Still, Ajay did know about Swing Dance Club somehow, so we can't be too careful. We've stopped going to that, though, both for that reason and because running into Mara right now would be a fairly unpleasant experience for everyone involved.

Send me a picture of him

I type back quickly. I spend a tense couple of minutes checking my phone every ten seconds. She's going to text me back and say that it was just a classmate. Or a TA. Or a Trick-or-Treater...on a college campus...in November. Normally it would just be someone fascinated by her eye color, but that wouldn't be the case this time because she's been wearing her brown contacts every day she's on campus lately. My phone vibrates and I jump.

"Are you okay?" asks Lindsay.

"Yes," I say, hoping that ends up being true. I look at the message. It's a picture. The part of the library she's in is fairly dark right now, so it's a little hard to make out. There are several rows of bookshelves to one side and a line of desks on the other, up against the wall. A few desks away from the camera is a figure in a hoodie. I squint at the screen, trying to make out the person's facial features. I shade the image with my hand and suddenly I can see it.

My blood runs cold.

It's definitely Ajay. Based on what I now know about Charlotte's past, I doubt he's there to reminisce about old times. She could be in very real danger. Normally, I'd just tell her to call the police, but she's never going to do that, not with whatever aversion she has to law enforcement. I glance over at Lindsay.

"What number presentation are we?"

"We're sixth," she says, eyeing me curiously.

At six minutes apiece, that's thirty-six minutes total, plus another couple of minutes or so for each group to set up. That puts us at about forty-eight minutes, towards the back of the order. A couple of months ago this situation would have completely paralyzed me. Even now, as I part my lips to say what I know I need to, it's not the easiest decision to make. But there's no way I'm going to sit back at let Ajay do his worst. That isn't who I am.

"There's a weird guy following one of my friends. I'll be right back."

I can't even bring myself to look them in the eyes as I say it. I just grab my backpack and run. The more time I spend explaining, the less time I have to get there and back again. I burst out of the door and almost bowl over the professor, who is on her way in to start the class. Luckily, I'm long gone into the sea of students before she turns around.

I dash down the stairs to the first floor, skidding a little at the bottom. It isn't until I'm outside again that think to text Charlotte.

Coming. Where in the library are you?

Then I'm off like a shot. Campus is busy enough at this hour to garner a few curious glances. It *is* close to the top of the hour, though, so most people assume I'm late for class. Which...I guess I am, technically.

Forty-eight minutes. That should be plenty of time, right? Campus isn't that big. I just need to get Charlotte out of there, maybe call the police if it comes to it, and then I'm back in time to give the presentation. Even given the seriousness of the situation, it strikes me as a bit poetic that this adventure started with me racing the clock to get to Swing Dance Club, and here I am doing it again for a very different reason. I also find it ironic that I went to so much effort to find Charlotte in the first place, and here this absolute bozo from her past traipses back in and randomly bumps into her at the library. There's no way I'm going to let him wreck everything she's fought so hard to build.

Ahead of me looms the library, emerging from the mist like the final boss from a video game. I crash through the entryway and whip out my phone to look at Charlotte's response. Except...it isn't there. That's worrying. I pull out the picture she sent. From the lighting, it's clear that it isn't any of the places in the library where we normally go. Where is it that dark? The basement, maybe?

I head down there. Unfortunately for me there are two levels of basement, and both of them are quite large. I start in the lowest one, flashing through row after row of periodicals. She's obviously somewhere quite secluded, so I have to be meticulous. Nothing would be worse than missing her completely and moving on to a different floor just because I overlooked the right nook. I scan through a mental map of the area. I think there are some weird desks pushed to the wall on the other side of the Norwegian section. My phone is still empty. Thirty-eight minutes remaining. That's still enough, surely? I run to the last place I can think of on this floor, but I can't go as fast as I'd like because my side is starting to cramp up. She's still not there.

The next level goes the same way: a relentless, furious search that makes me feel like Charlotte has suddenly vanished into thin air and that I'll be destined to search endless labyrinths of library shelves for her for all of eternity, like some kind of off-brand Greek myth. Still nothing from her. There are thirty-two minutes left.

Having ransacked the entire basement, I have no choice but to keep going even though I'm not sure which other parts of the library would be as dark as it was in the picture. I hope against hope that she's not responding because she hasn't seen my text yet, not because something happened to her. Although you'd think it'd be hard to get away with much in a building full of students and faculty.

The fire in my lungs is forcing me to slow down a little. I think about the look on Raymond's face if I don't make it back in time and push a little harder. My group members should honestly still be fine even if I don't make it back. They can give their part of the presentation and throw me to the wolves. That might actually help their chances of getting a good score because the professor is less likely to dock them for parts I might have missed. Still, I don't want to let them down.

That said, Charlotte's safety comes first. It occurs to me, as I finish scouring the ground level and move up to the second floor, that it's a little odd how much power school has over people. It's supposed to be this sacrosanct vehicle that gets me to a better place in life, but here it is making it harder to prioritize what really matters. I'm not about to let Charlotte get hurt over a single letter on a transcript somewhere to get into a career that I honestly don't even care much about. Higher education is a powerful tool, but like any tool, it's only as useful as it is applied wisely.

I finish searching the second floor and check the time. Twenty-five minutes left. Wait! There's a message from Charlotte.

Top floor. Northeast corner. Hurry.

Hurry. My legs find new life as I sprint up the stairs, calculating that the elevator will take me longer. Which way is northeast, again?

I have no clue, so I just run until I find an outside wall and follow it around the edge of the building. There's one corner. Two. That way leads to the annex, which is on the south end. Three. This should be it up ahead. It isn't dimly lit at all. That makes me hesitate a half-second. Then I see that blonde hair with the slightest of waves to it poking out from behind a desk. I've found her. She must have gotten nervous and moved to a place with more people around.

Where's Ajay?

I put my head on a swivel. Is he behind me, by any chance? No, I don't see him. Where's that hoodie?

As soon as I think this, I see it emerge from behind a row of bookshelves up ahead between Charlotte and me. Ajay. He's walking swiftly toward her, reaching for her shoulder. Not on my watch. I close the gap and pile drive into his back, sending him flying. He hits the ground hard.

Charlotte. I find her with one hand and move her behind me, eyes fixed on Ajay. He pops up and immediately throws an elbow strike to my face. I jerk backwards and feel the breeze from the sudden movement kiss my face as it misses by a hairsbreadth. If I had any doubts about his intentions, they've now been bashed to pieces with a sledgehammer, although why he's choosing now to get violent instead of running away like he did last time, I can't fathom. I guess he assumes that if he doesn't take me out right now, we're going to nab him once and for all. Well, he isn't wrong.

I make a quick calculation. If I run right now, I might be able to escape to a more crowded area, but I can't do that with Charlotte with me. That means I need to stall until someone figures out what's happening and gets help. I throw a right hook towards Ajay's jaw, but he ducks under it like a prizefighter and counters with a left that sends me into the desk behind me. There's fire in his eyes.

"Call the police!" I finally have the presence of mind to yell to Charlotte. I don't want this to get too dangerous, so I grab several books from the shelf next to me and thrust them into his face, hoping to blind him long enough for us to escape. A particularly large one hits him right in the sunglasses and knocks him back half a step. He bats it away with one hand and socks me in the face with a well-oiled strike with the other that sends me reeling. I bring my arms up instinctively to protect my face, and he immediately punches me in the stomach. He's breaking me down with clinical precision. I'm no match for him.

"Run!" I call back to Charlotte as I take another blow to the side of my head. I'm done for. The only fortunate thing about the barrage of fists he's unleashing on me is that it doesn't give me time to consider the precious seconds slipping away until the presentation.

Charlotte yells something, but I can't tell what it is because I'm busy trying to get hit as little as possible. There's a deep ferocity to Ajay's movements that fills me with primal terror. Am I going to get seriously hurt from this?

Then I remember who's standing behind me. I may not be able to beat Ajay, but if I can keep him from hurting Charlotte, it doesn't matter. I can still protect her.

My fear evaporates. I drop my guard and punch Ajay as hard as I can, throwing caution to the wind. As he's recovering from that, I wrench the desk next to me between us, creating a physical barrier while I pelt him with more books. With my free hand, I push Charlotte a step back from me, trying to get her to make a break for it. She isn't moving for some reason. In front of me, Ajay hits a new level of rage. He vaults over the desk and tackles me, knocking me flat on my back.

I'm done for. Strangely, I'm still not afraid. I cover my head and neck with my arms the best I can and wait for it to end. Hopefully someone will intervene before it's too late. My vision swims. The last thing I see before I black out is Charlotte stepping over me.

I sure hope she knows what she's doing, is my last thought as consciousness fades.

Chapter 28

I stare down at the toy in my hand. It's a plastic dinosaur egg, one of the ones you used to get in kid's meals back in the day. The idea was to crack it open and dig through the small mound of kinetic sand inside to reveal a baby dinosaur. I turn it over in my hands, eyes wide with excitement. This is the very coolest thing I've owned in some time. In fact, right at that moment, it feels like the coolest thing I've ever owned.

I glance around surreptitiously, but my dad's still in the bathroom, so I hastily open it up and set to work on excavating the dinosaur. If I hurry I might have just enough time--

"What are you doing?"

I look up to see my father looming over me far too soon. How did he finish so fast? I instinctively try to hide the dinosaur egg, but that only makes it more obvious what I've been up to.

"Why are you wasting time playing with that?" Dad asks brusquely. Even though it's a memory from some time ago, his mannerisms are uncannily similar to what they are today.

Staring up into his unsympathetic face, my initial excitement wilts and starts to fade.

"How are you going to become a doctor when you waste your time playing with silly toys?"

I look down at the toy again, but now it's all ruined. Despite my best efforts, with those few words from my father, I suddenly I can't see it as anything but a waste of space. When nobody's looking, I dump it in the nearest trashcan.

* * *

The concrete ceiling that stares down at me when I open my eyes is as cold and unwelcoming a sight as I've ever seen. That was it. That was the memory that had been burgeoning inside of me since that one conversation with Charlotte. The day I lost my childlike sense of wonder. It strikes me as ironic that becoming a doctor was the thing my father used to try to whip me into shape. I guess he didn't realize how expensive medical school was at that point.

Anyway, concrete ceiling. For the first time, I realize that this is strange because the library has ceiling tiles. I'm blissfully ignorant of the implications of this for a few more seconds because my body is aching everywhere bodies can ache. Then I put two and two together. Foreign environment plus bodily injury means I'm in the hospital. That's somewhat of a good sign because it means that someone who doesn't want me dead must have intervened to bring me here.

Speaking of dead things, my medical career is in more dire need of an undertaker than Charlotte's roommate. I hope Raymond and Lindsay did okay without me. I suppose being in the hospital might be enough of a reason for the professor to give me another shot, but based on her reputation, I doubt it. Just a few hours before (Yesterday? This morning? I have no idea what time it is), medical school was around the corner for me. Now the entire course of my future has changed. I lie there for a minute, letting what used to be my dream disperse into the ether. Well, good riddance. I'd rather have that regret than sit back and let Charlotte get beat up.

There's an odd clanging sound.

"Wake up! Everyone wake up!"

That's a peculiar way for hospital staff to behave. I sit up, and a blistering headache rocks my world. It almost makes me lie back down again, but I need to ask the nurses about Charlotte while they're still here.

I blink slowly, looking in the direction of the noise. All I see is an iron door that looks like it was built to withstand Goliath. There are no nurses to be seen. Confused, I make my way over to the door and pull on it. It doesn't budge. This hospital...locks their patients in? I peer out the window, which is also a fairly odd addition for a hospital room. I don't see any nurses, just a security guard of some kind walking down the hall and banging on each door in turn.

Huh? Then I look down at myself and see an orange jumpsuit. It finally hits me: I'm not in the hospital. I'm in jail. The person I thought was a security guard was actually a corrections officer. I panic.

Suddenly the room feels the size of a shoebox, and I have a mental image of being trapped here for the rest of my life, subsisting on army rations and mystery meat, never to see the outside world again. My heart pounds, and my breathing gets shallow. Is this what Charlotte feels like every time she has a panic attack? I instinctively reach for my phone, but it isn't there. I'm cut off from the outside world.

"Did you just try the door?"

A cacophony of laughter assaults my ears. For the first time, I realize that I am not alone. My two bunkmates are beside themselves with mirth over the inmate who had the gall to try the door to his jail cell. I lie back down on the bed and try to ignore them. This is going to be a long day.

After what feels like eons, the door opens. It's a guard.

"Simmons?"

I raise a hand, and he beckons for me to come with him. He leads me down the hall to another door.

"Booking, please," he says into the radio. There's a clicking sound and the door unlocks. On the other side is an open area with an adjoining office.

"Today's your lucky day," the guard tells me. "The kid you hit decided not to press charges."

I can tell from the way he says this that he deeply disagrees with the decision. I'm too relieved to be offended. But...why did Ajay come at me with such intensity only to suddenly let it go? And why am *I* the one who ended up in here? I don't have time to dwell on this, though, because I have to figure out how to get home from here.

They give me back my clothes and other belongings, and I head out into the lobby. I was in jail for just a few hours, most of which I spent unconscious, but it's still a weight off my shoulders when I take my first breath of fresh air. I never want to go back there ever again. I feel beaten up as much mentally as I am physically. Anyway, it will all be much better once I see Charlotte's face. My phone rings several times, and I start to worry that I'll have to get a ride from Micah.

"Hello?"

"It's me." I say.

"Levi!"

I smile a little in spite of myself.

"Can you come get me?"

"Sure thing!"

"Thank you." My voice breaks a little.

"Are you okay?"

"Are you?"

"Yes."

"Then yes."

"That was so sweet, I'm going to have to brush my teeth after this."

"You'd better get used to having a clean mouth,
then."

"'K, I'll be there in a bit."

"'K."

"Love you."

"Love you too."

I see a familiar gray car pull up through the window
and am out the door like a shot. Then I regret it
immediately as my head begins to pound again like a
hammer striking an anvil. Charlotte emerges from the car
and rushes over to me, arms outstretched. This time I'm
the one who collapses into them instead of the other way
around.

"You're really okay?" I ask. "How did you get away?
Do you have some kind of superpower I don't know
about?"

She nods.

"I can see the possible versions of the future. It's
actually really easy because they all have you in it."

I push her gently on the shoulder.

"Seriously, how did you get away?"

"Well, actually..."

It's then that I notice the other person getting out of
the car. Ajay.

If it wasn't for what the guard said earlier about him
not pressing charges, I would have leapt out of my skin.
As it is, I'm still awfully confused.

"Get in the car," says Charlotte. "We owe you an
explanation."

"It's time for me to tell you my story," says Charlotte.
After some discussion about the best place for privacy,
we're sitting in the car in the parking lot of a large retail
store.

"Didn't you already do that before?" I say.

"Those were the highlights. There were some things I didn't mention. I never told you *why* I ran away from the group home in the first place."

That's true. It makes me wonder what else she left out.

"Why did you?"

Charlotte pauses, and it's clear she's having difficulty getting the words out.

"You can do it," says Ajay supportively. My eyes flick between the two of them.

"The group home we went to was abusive," she chokes out.

The group home that *we* went to.

"Abusive how?"

"When we broke their rules, they would put us in a room by ourselves and just—scream at us until we promised not to do it again. They told us awful things like that it was our fault we couldn't be with our parents because we were such bad kids. At first we didn't believe them, but after being told that over and over, it was hard not to. Then we would get angry at them and act out on purpose, and they would point to that as proof that they were right about us being horrible."

Ajay nods, remembering. Charlotte continues.

"Sometimes they would hit us, but they made sure never to leave a mark in case one of us told on them. Some of us tried, but they pretended like we were making stuff up to get out of consequences for acting out, and the staff would all back each other up, but we never could do the same because that would make us a rat and we all knew that was dangerous."

So this is where her panic attacks came from. Being screamed at like that over and over, especially as a child who was still in the process of building her concept of the world, would scar anyone in one way or another.

"Eventually I couldn't take it anymore, and I ran away. I couldn't go to my parents, or the authorities would send me right back."

"And that's how you ended up on the streets."

"That's how I ended up on the streets."

That all makes sense, but how does that add up to worrying that someone was after her? Surely the group home can't take her back now that she's an adult.

"How does Ajay come into this?"

"He started living there right after they sent me back from the streets. His home life wasn't as bad as the rest of us, so he had a hard time adjusting to what they were doing to us."

I hold up a hand.

"You're saying that everyone in the group home grew up in such awful environments that they *were used* to being treated that way?"

"Yeah,"

"And you not only survived it but managed to get into college afterwards?"

"...Yeah."

"I think you were lying about not having superpowers."

"I didn't say that! I said--" She glances surreptitiously at Ajay. "Never mind. Anyway, Ajay wasn't used to it, so he was pushing back a lot more than the other kids. We got to be friends, and I'd always go talk to him through the door if they left him alone too long. Well, one day he pushed back a little *too* hard, and the director flipped his lid and actually hurt him."

My eyes shift to the scar on Ajay's chin.

"The group home staff got all scared that they were going to get found out and swore us to secrecy. They tried to patch him up themselves, even though it was obvious that he needed medical attention. So--" her eyes drop, "I told on them."

"Is that...a bad thing?" I'm confused by the mixed messaging.

"He looked to me like he lost a lot of blood, but it actually wasn't even close to life threatening. The group home had to shut down, and because child protective services had to scramble to find placements for so many minors, a lot of kids ended up in even worse situations because the foster families weren't vetted properly."

"Worse than being hit and screamed at all the time?"

She and Ajay share a look.

"Yes." She doesn't elaborate. "Everyone in the group home lost their jobs. I didn't realize until afterward, but a lot of the staff didn't even know what was going on, and there were a few others who knew and didn't say anything but tried to make it easier on the kids."

"What happened to you?"

"I was one of the lucky ones who got a good foster family. They taught me how to function in society and even adopted me. I went to therapy for a while, and that helped some, but I could never get over the guilt of how many lives I ruined."

"You saved all the kids since then that would have ended up there but got better placements instead!"

She nods.

"My counselor always told me that. It makes sense, but I've never been able to get myself to believe it."

"Wait, you've been to therapy, so why do you still have panic attacks?"

She looks at me like I'm an innocent young pup.

"Therapy is a lot of work. Your problems don't disappear just because you talk to someone. You have to put in a lot of effort outside of the session for it to do much. Also, to be honest, I never told my therapist the whole story. I lied to him to get out of coming."

"You weren't ready to face that part at that point."

"I was childish."

I open my mouth again to argue the point, but I can see that it won't get me anywhere.

"So what does all of that have to do with wearing brown contacts and jumping at shadows?"

"I got a lot of death threats after the group home shut down. I was never sure whether it was employees of the group home or some of the residents who were gang affiliated. It got so bad at one point that my adoptive family had to move. A couple of years afterward someone broke into our house and tore it apart."

"Seriously? And it was definitely connected to the group home?"

"They left a picture of me with the eyes scribbled out next to a dead rat."

"That would do it."

"That's when I started to wear contacts to make my eyes look brown. It's always been the thing that stands out about me the most, so it's the first thing they'd look for."

"But you weren't wearing contacts the first time I met you. Or when we went on that date."

At the word "date," Ajay's brow furrows.

"I don't really know why I didn't wear them then. I guess I was starting to feel like it had been so long that people had started to forget."

I turn on Ajay.

"So if you knew all this, why were you being so creepy about trying to find her? You made me think *you* were the one after her."

"Ah, well, to be honest I found a picture of you with Charlotte on a date on social media and thought you looked like one of the staff members' kids, so I thought if I was sneakier about finding her..."

I raise my eyebrows.

"I think we can rule out a future in the CIA for you, buddy."

Then it hits me. All this time I thought I was protecting Charlotte, but I was actually getting all riled up over something that wasn't even a real threat. *This* is what I gave up medical school for, a total sham.

I feel a sudden flash of anger toward Ajay. If he had just *communicated*, none of this would have happened. Although I suppose the same could be said about me. True, Charlotte had fed me that line about not wanting to know who she had to forgive, but I could have insisted. And I never gave Ajay the chance to say his piece in the library. I just attacked him. I feel extraordinarily dumb right now.

"So it probably *is* the case that people have forgotten what happened."

"Maybe," says Charlotte. "You came rolling in like the headless horseman was after you, though, so I wasn't going to question you on it."

"I made you worried over nothing."

She shrugs. "We made it through. It's chill."

I suddenly understand what Charlotte was saying a minute ago about having a hard time letting reassurances sink in. I still feel ridiculously guilty, even though she's obviously over it. Suddenly I just want to go home. Charlotte seems to see it on my face.

"Let's get you out of here," she says.

"Before those coppers change their minds about letting you out," says Ajay.

Charlotte laughs harder than I've seen from her in a long time, and I feel an unmistakable sting of jealousy.

No. I shake my head. *He's her childhood friend. I'm not going to let my own pettiness get in the way.*

"Yeah, let's do that. I want to leave all this behind me as soon as possible."

Chapter 29

When we get home, Charlotte drops me off, and she and Ajay head off to get ice cream. An odd choice after picking a friend up from jail, but it's not like I have much experience with such things. Also, it does make sense that they'd want to chat a bit after seeing each other for the first time in five years. At least, that's what I try to tell myself.

Micah leaps up from the couch as soon as I open the door.

"Where were you?"

"Ah." I don't want to lie, but I also don't want to get into it right now.

"I was—out."

"You were gone over twenty-four hours. A couple of your classmates came by they said you missed the final presentation so they ended up having to present without the slides and bombed it."

The revelation hits me like a freight train. They didn't have the slides? Then I remember. *I* was the one with the flash drive. Not only did I go chasing after Charlotte about a threat that turned out to be her best friend in disguise, I managed to crater Raymond's and Lindsay's futures in one fell swoop. I am the absolute scum of the earth. The more I think about it, the more ridiculous it seems. Charlotte's a college student. She isn't going around getting chased by an international terrorist group! I've ruined everything for everybody over something that didn't even exist to start with.

In front of me, Micah is still waiting expectantly.

"I messed up."

"Well mess up when you don't have people staying up all night worrying about you."

I see the bags under his eyes and the guilt intensifies.

"Sorry."

"Sorry isn't good enough."

I want to curl up into a tiny ball and disappear. My head starts pounding again.

"I thought that Charlotte was in trouble."

"So you went and hit someone? And then he was too much for you to handle and wrote you a one-way ticket to the ER," he says eyeing my banged up face.

I didn't correct him on the ER piece because that would only make it worse.

"Levi, when will you learn not to mess with things you don't understand?" Micah doesn't even try to hide his frustration.

"I thought it was the best way to help her."

"Then she would be better off without you."

Normally I would have shrugged this off, but today I find myself believing him.

"You're right."

Micah gives me an odd look.

"That's the first time."

"The first time what?"

"The first time you've admitted when you were wrong."

Something in me starts to crack. Actually, it's a crack that's been slowly forming for a while now, but suddenly it's as wide as a chasm. I should never have gotten myself involved with Charlotte. I've broken things wherever I've gone. Mara, Raymond, Lindsay, Micah, myself, I've majorly wrecked things for all of them. And with how dependent on me Charlotte's been getting, it looks like she's next on the list. I remember Mara's warning: "Don't let her ruin your life, Levi." Only Charlotte didn't have to do anything. I can take care of the ruining all on my own.

Even Micah seems to realize I've reached my limit and leaves me alone. I disappear into my room, shut the door behind me, and collapse onto my bed. My mattress is soooo comfortable. At least I can count on one thing in my life not to disappear on me. I'll be able to put the pieces back together somehow, right? Maybe I can talk to the professor and get her to raise Raymond's and Lindsay's grades since I'm the only reason they failed. I'll probably also need to look into changing my major at some point. Maybe I can find something I actually *want* to do instead of something I see as an obligation.

My phone buzzes. I grab it happily, thinking it's Charlotte. It isn't. In fact, it isn't even a text message. It's an email from the school. The subject line reads: "Formal Notice of Disciplinary Hearing." I open it with trepidation.

"*Dear Levi Simmons,*" it begins. "*This notice is to inform you of a written complaint from library staff related to a serious altercation on campus. The complaint alleges that you violently assaulted a campus guest without provocation. An investigation is ongoing. You will be contacted again when your hearing has been scheduled.*"

My arms fall to my side. They can't throw me out for this, can they? Surely once they hear Ajay explain the misunderstanding, they'll let me walk. There's been a lot of fear over the last couple of days, but the variety that grips me now is a whole level darker. I look down at the mattress beneath me. This...*isn't* going to disappear on me, right? What on Earth have I gotten myself into?

* * *

238

The next morning Charlotte doesn't show up at my door for the first time in weeks. That's a shame because I really need her today. I feel the chasm inside of me start to widen even further at her absence. I almost text her but eventually decide that I don't want to be a bother. She has enough to worry about.

It's a real fight getting myself out of the door. What's the use of going to class if I'm going to get expelled in a couple of weeks? What's the use of going to campus if Charlotte isn't going to be there? In the end, the main reason I finally sling my backpack over my shoulder and head out is because if I don't maintain some semblance of normalcy, I'm afraid I'll fall apart completely.

It's a full-on battle to pay attention in class. *It's not all that likely that I'm actually getting kicked out* I remind myself. That's not how it feels, though.

The routine has been to catch Charlotte after her first class of the day and go somewhere to study, usually the library. There's a part of me that's irrationally nervous that she won't be there because she didn't come with me to campus this morning. It feels like she'll have dropped off of the face of the Earth for some reason, never to be seen again. I'm sure to get to the room a couple of minutes early and breathe a sigh of relief as soon as I see those purple eyes.

"You aren't wearing your contacts," I notice.

"I wouldn't want the world to miss out on these beauties," she says, tapping her face, and suddenly everything is right with the world. Well, mostly. I almost ask her about why she wasn't there this morning, but there doesn't seem to be a reason to bother with that now that everything's back to normal.

"What's crackin'?" she asks me.

I consider telling her about the disciplinary hearing, but it's a painful thought that I don't want to get into right now. So instead I say:

"Just happy to see you."

Her face brightens at that, and we head for the library. We settle down in one of our usual spots that's far enough away from everything else that we can get away with a little quiet conversation.

"How was catching up with Ajay?" I ask once we're settled.

"*So* nice. He's got so much rizz. Oh! Get this! He says that he has some connections at a record label and might be able to introduce me to some people in the music industry."

"Wow!" I say. There's a mix of genuine happiness for her as well as a little guilty disappointment that the thing that's finally breaking through for her isn't anything I've done. Also, the prospect of her spending a lot more time with Ajay in the near future isn't exactly thrilling. I shake my head. Get it together, Levi! This could be a life-changing opportunity for her.

The conversation hums on. *At least Ajay doesn't go to this school,* I think.

But at lunchtime when we make our way to our usual picnic table, Ajay is there waiting for us.

"I invited him," says Charlotte.

"Great," I say again as sincerely as I can manage.

Ajay is actually quite a nice guy when you get to know him. He apologizes for the shiners he left on my face even though it was my misunderstanding that led to them. He gets Charlotte laughing pretty much every other sentence. I finally bring up the disciplinary hearing because he's probably the only person on the planet who can help me.

"For sure I'll be there," he says. "I'll give you my number, and you can hit me up when you know the day."

That softens my attitude toward him a little.

"Anything else I can do to help?" he asks.

"The other things I have to take care of only I can do," I say. "I've got to talk to my O-Chem professor and try to get her to raise my group members' scores."

My voice cracks a little involuntarily as I say that.

"Are you really okay?" asks Charlotte. I sigh. I can't lie to her, especially after I've worked so hard to get her to be open herself.

"It just feels like I've been messing things up for everyone lately. First Mara, then my group members. It's a reverse Midas touch. Everything I come into contact with turns to dirt."

"Hang on! That isn't fair! Those things only happened because you were trying to help me."

"Which I screwed up royally."

"You didn't know that when you were doing it."

"That's what makes it so awful."

"*You*," she says waving a finger in my face, "cannot take a compliment. What, are you allergic to them now?"

I take a bite of sandwich to avoid answering.

"You're only paying attention to the negative side," she continues. "You're dismissing anything that could remotely be considered positive about what you've accomplished."

"Sounds like someone else I know," interjects Ajay.

Charlotte freezes. A strange look comes over her face.

"You're right," she says slowly. She's suddenly deep in thought.

I look on in shock. After weeks of me trying desperately to drill that very idea into her head, *that's* what does it? Ajay utters a single sentence, and instantly she can see the light? It's oddly uncomfortable to see him slowly becoming Charlotte's hero. I should just be happy for her, but I can't quite bring myself to be, at least not completely.

"I get now why people always get so frustrated at me because of that," she adds. "I've been shutting down the positive feedback people give me my whole life."

"Well, maybe now's a good time to stop," says Ajay. My chasm grows a little wider.

* * *

I wait patiently for Charlotte at the normal spot after classes are done. She's slightly later than normal, and when she does arrive, she has bad news. Well, it's actually good news, technically, but right now it doesn't feel that way.

"Ajay's taking me to see one of his music industry contacts," she says excitedly.

"Great! Have a good time," I say, not even able to make eye contact with her. It's not her success itself that I'm upset about. It's the way I'm starting to feel like an afterthought.

I trudge home by myself. The loneliness that creeps in is somehow more powerful than the kind that always seemed to be there before I met Charlotte. No one's home when I get there, so I actually do homework out of desperation to take my mind off of Ajay. Also, because with the promise of his help, I feel a lot better about my chances of staying in school, so maybe it's worth it to keep putting effort in. Augh! There he goes, worming his way into my thoughts again. It's strange to think that only a couple of days ago, he was enemy number one. There's a tiny part of me I'm ashamed of that wishes he still was.

The rest of the day drags on. My apartment stays silent. Because I'm trying so hard to distract myself, I get a fair amount of homework done. Still, when I turn in for bed, there's one prevailing thought: I hope things are better tomorrow.

* * *

Charlotte doesn't show up again the following morning. I text her and head to campus. Today her first class doesn't finish until after mine starts, so she's always waiting for me when I get out. Except today she isn't. I'm not surprised, but I am disappointed. So instead of hanging out with her, I head to my O-Chem professor's office in an effort to convince her to change my group members' grades. After hearing my explanation, she says that she'll think about bumping up Lindsay's and Raymond's scores, but she won't budge at all when it comes to my own.

"Because ending up in jail was a result of your own actions, I will not be changing your grade one point," she tells me.

I'm not surprised, but there's something about hearing it from her that makes the chasm inside me continue its outward expansion.

I find Charlotte again after her second class. She seems happy to see me, so I don't bring up not meeting me after my class earlier. Instead I ask her how the meeting with Ajay's contact went.

"You won't believe it. You *will* not believe it."

I steel myself. I'm *going* to be happy for her, whatever it is, I promise myself.

"They want to sign me to their record label!"

"What? Wait, who was this music contact?"

"I guess it's someone who's friends with the owner."

"And they signed you just like that?"

"They want to. They had me sing a few things for them, and it sounds like they were really impressed.

They even told me to send them a single as soon as I can get one ready."

She doesn't need me anymore. She never needed me. All she ever needed was Ajay, my mind contributes unhelpfully. I take a deep breath and remind myself of everything Charlotte's been through, of how hard she has fought to get here.

"I guess you're going to be able to share your light with a lot of people now," I tell her.

She nods enthusiastically.

"I probably won't be able to hang out anymore because I'll be working on my music so much."

"Right."

It isn't her words themselves that bother me, it's the fact that, from her tone, she doesn't seem to care one way or another that there won't be a place for me in her life anymore. Didn't I mean more to her than that? She's supposed to be the special one, the person who turns my life inside out and finally tells me what it all means. Why's she acting like none of that matters? It feels like my entire life is crumbling to pieces around me, and the one person I thought I could count on to help me through it doesn't seem to have any idea how much I'm struggling. I almost say something to that effect, but I don't want to rain on Charlotte's parade, especially today, so I bite my tongue.

The rest of the day is fairly normal, with the exception that Ajay comes and whisks her away again in the afternoon to work on a vocal track to send to the executive because they need to "strike while the iron's hot."

He's not wrong.

I give up. I think as I trudge home. If Charlotte doesn't want to spend time with me, I can't force her. It's all I can do to try to keep the battered pieces of my life together as much as possible, but I can't help but feel that I'm fighting a losing battle. Once again my apartment is empty. Hopefully that means that the disasters are over for the day.

Unfortunately for me, that doesn't end up being true. In fact, I've only been home for about twenty minutes before I receive the text that is going to send my entire life, which is already bursting at the seams, into a full-on tailspin.

Chapter 30

The text is from Charlotte:

I'm getting evicted

It takes me a few passes before I gather what's happening. I breathe slowly in and out, trying to stop my chest from caving in.

Levi, I have to have a mailing address for the record label to send the contract to

That makes sense. Having a reliable way of contacting her would be a must for something like this. Then the third text comes in.

Can you help me?

She's asking for help. Charlotte's actually asking for help with money. That gives me a sense of how desperate she is, of how much this means to her.

I undoubtedly have enough money in my account to cover whatever that anthill of an apartment is going to run for the month. The issue is that if I use it on this, my father is going to *flip his lid*. The account is entirely in my name, so I wouldn't be breaking any laws if I use it. The issue is that if I pay for Charlotte's rent, there's a decent chance that my father will literally disown me. Maybe if I get a loan in my name using what's in my account now as collateral, or maybe I could just—I stop. I just stop. I hit some invisible limit that I didn't realize was there. For a long time now, I've been stretching, stretching, stretching, cracking, cracking, cracking, but now I'm not just cracked, I'm broken.

I collapse onto the couch.

Down the hall a door opens. Surprised, I sit up. It was so quiet when I arrived that I was sure I was alone. It's Micah. He surveys my prostrate position with a knowing look.

"This is what you get for not approaching situations rationally."

I just look up at him. I don't have the energy to argue.

"Are you going to keep going like this until you've thrown your whole life away? Or are you going to stop lying to yourself and face reality?"

"What does that even mean?" I snap.

"What?"

"What does it even mean to approach this rationally?"

"It means to stop chasing after fantasies and be serious about your life for once."

"But what does that *mean*? You're always spouting these platitudes about being logical and using your brain, but *what am I supposed to do*? Am I just supposed to logic my tuition money for next semester into my bank account?"

"If you had stayed away from that girl to start with, that wouldn't even be a question."

In my heart of hearts I don't believe him, but I'm so beaten down that I have a hard time shaking it off the way I normally do. Befriending Charlotte was the right decision. It *has* to be. Because if it wasn't, what am I left with?

If it was such a good decision, then why has she abandoned you? the Micah in my head chimes in to tag team with his corporal counterpart. *If you meant anything to her, she would have*—The thought is interrupted by yet another door opening down the hall. Great, Chris is here too? Just what I need, someone else to join the dogpile. Then I see the silhouette in the doorway.

"I don't normally get involved in these types of conversations," Mason says, and I swear his T-shirt looks like shining armor. "But I think it's time for me to step in."

"This doesn't concern you," says Micah.

"Doesn't it?" He looks over at me. "Maybe not. I don't care. I've tried to make it a habit of mine to try to put good into the world as much as I can. Who knows? Maybe a miracle will happen."

Micah makes a dismissive sound but turns to face him nonetheless.

Micah and Mason circle each other, like gladiators preparing for a death match. They're feeling each other out. Testing. Probing. The very air hums with their electricity. Micah strikes first.

"A miracle, huh? Believing in miracles is the way that people comfort themselves in knowing that one day they won't be here anymore. They try to slap a smiley face sticker onto everything because they're not willing to face the truth."

"If you dive deeply enough, every philosophical argument is based on assumptions," Mason counters. "You should know that better than anyone. Believing in the lack of miracles is as much of an assumption as believing in their existence."

"So you admit you don't have any proof."

To my surprise, Mason nods.

"God created the world such that one person could look at the night sky and see Him everywhere, and someone else could look at the same sky and see Him nowhere. And because of that, what we choose to believe about miracles says more about *us* than it does about Him. Look--"

Mason grabs one of Micah's philosophy textbooks from off the table and flips open the table of contents.

"For thousands of years, people a lot smarter than you and I have spent their whole lives trying to understand existence through pure reason. And every one of them--" He taps the portrait of each philosopher in turn, "came up with *completely* different answers. Which shows that logic alone isn't enough to understand life."

Micah blinks irritably at Mason's implicit suggestion that he isn't as smart as Plato before firing back:

"Better logic than pure madness!"

"Hey, I'm not saying logic is useless, it's still important. What I'm saying is that we need both our mind--" He reaches out one had in a cupping shape, "and our heart--" he grabs it with his other hand, making a miniature yin-yang symbol, "to get a complete picture of what life's about."

"Making decisions emotionally isn't going to get you anywhere." Mason shakes his head.

"It isn't about emotion. It's about love."

Micah rolls his eyes.

"I'm serious," Mason continues. "Love isn't an emotion. There's a feeling that comes with it, sure, but it's much more than that. It's sacrifice. Dedication. Loyalty. It's fighting with your whole heart for something bigger than yourself. It's letting go of your own interests until there's nothing left. But it's also not something that is possible to pin down through logic alone. There isn't a single action that is always loving in any single case. And there is no action that, in the right circumstances, can never be loving. Because of that, it is something that must be believed, not proven. Love *itself* is a miracle."

Micah makes a dismissive sound.

"I don't expect to convince you," says Mason. "You're really not actually the one I'm talking to." He turns to me.

"Miracles are real, and they start inside you. They start by choosing to love, to *really* love, not just to experience strong emotions, not just to repress things that you want out of guilt or pity or duty. It isn't enough to call something love because everyone else calls it that. It isn't enough to call it love just because there's some type of connection or attachment. Real love is deeper than all of those things. It is reaching a point where you want another person's happiness more than you want your own. It's giving them your all and holding nothing back. It's focusing the whole of your existence on a single point and letting your life and theirs fill with light. It's all that and more. There's something about it that transcends and defies all attempts to describe it, which is exactly what makes it so beautiful. That is why it is to be believed rather than proven."

Mason walks up to me and takes me by the shoulders.

"Whatever you're going through, don't give up on love. If you lose everything else in your life but still have that, you have a treasure more precious than what most people in this world will ever know. To love is to become fully independent of all of your circumstances, to become unconditional. It is the greatest joy that can ever be experienced, but the irony of it is that as you get there and when you get there, that is never the point. The point is always, *always* the wellbeing of the person you love.

"When you love like that, your fear falls away, and you begin to see beneath the surface of this fallen world. You begin to see things that you can't put words to. And then it becomes obvious that all of these ideas," he waves vaguely in the direction of Micah, "don't matter much. Love isn't to be understood in some abstract way in a textbook. It is to be lived. Love isn't just a miracle, it is *the* miracle, and all other miracles in life, big or small, stem from it."

I look up to see that Mason's eyes are full of tears.

"The irony about you having the gall to dismiss every philosopher in history is that you sound an awful lot like Soren Kierkegaard right now," says Micah.

"Kierkegaard was a man who understood that actions speak louder than words and that philosophers are bound by that as much as anyone else. What good has this philosophy of yours actually done, Micah? When has it actually made people's lives any better than they were before they interacted with it? Has it made your life better?" he asks me.

I shake my head without thinking twice.

"Saying that your love is the real deal and that everyone else's is a sham is the height of arrogance," says Micah.

"Love is like a lump of gold ore," Mason returns, pulling a shiny rock from his pocket. Micah and I both give him a look.

"I use this with couples clients a lot," he explains sheepishly. "Anyway, just like this rock, most love is a mixture of genuine care for the beloved and self-interest. Even diluted love is extraordinarily powerful. If someone walked up to you on the street and gave you a lump of gold ore, you wouldn't say 'ew, no thanks, why isn't this twenty-four karat?' You'd be amazed that someone was willing to give you something this valuable. At the same time, the more impurities are purged from love, the more valuable it becomes. Eventually, just as pure gold is quite different than the ore it comes from, it reaches an inflection point at which it transforms from something valuable but ordinary into something miraculous."

Micah makes another dismissive sound.

"I can sense a lot of pain in you," says Mason to Micah. "I don't know what it's from, but I can tell that you hold onto a lot of anger toward the world because of it. I think that's why you gravitate toward this type of philosophy: because it's your way of dealing with the bitterness you've experienced. I don't fault you for that, but for someone who goes on and on about self-honesty, it seems like there's room for more introspection in your life as well."

For once, Micah is silent.

"I can't tell you what the solutions to your problems are because I don't know them well enough to be able to," he says, turning back to me, "but if you make your decisions out of love the way I've described it, you're going to figure it out somehow. And it might not look like how you'd think. Sometimes the quietest acts of love are the greatest."

With that, he disappears back into his room. Micah stands there for a minute more. Then he walks over to Mason's door and knocks on it. Mason lets him in, and I can hear the quiet murmuring of continued conversation from behind the door.

I look down at my hands. Make my decision out of love, huh? A fat lot of good that's done me. Yet there's something about the way Mason said it that resonates with me. It strikes me that he was trying to practice what he preaches. He talked about love and bringing good into the world, and he tried to do it in a way that built us up, even Micah. I think there is a part of Micah that does mean well, but the intention of his debates is to dominate, control, and tear down, rather than to build something better than was there before. I finally understand why Micah's way of approaching life bothers me so much. It's not because I'm in denial, it's because I want to be the type of person that tries to bring out the best in people.

Which is exactly what Mason just said love is, I think. And that's really what my relationship with Charlotte has always been about: helping her overcome her panic attacks and reach her potential as a singer. Only recently, I've let jealousy and self pity upstage all of that. It sucks that my only friend is starting to drift away from me, but does that really affect what I do here? So what if Ajay swoops in and sweeps her off her feet? So what if Charlotte forgets about me? That was never the point. I got involved because I wanted to make life better for her, and it looks like here's my chance.

I love Charlotte, I've known that for some time. The question life seems to be asking me is this: I love her enough to give up my dignity, my financial stability, even my college career for her, but do I love deeply enough, sincerely enough, truly enough, to risk losing my relationship with my dad?

It takes me several hours to come up with an answer to that question. It isn't because I don't know what the answer is going to be. It's because that even knowing it, the actual choosing of it is excruciating.

In reality, it isn't actually my relationship with my father that I'm sacrificing. If I'm being honest, that has been shriveling for a long time now. It's giving up the hope for it to be more than a superficial pretending, an awkward dance where we both step on each other's toes in time to the music, at least on my time table. It's shutting the door and handing him the key.

Mason is right, the important thing is to let love be my guide. My life will carry on, even if Dad cuts me off completely. I'll figure out some way of moving forward.

What can't be replaced is this chance for Charlotte to leave her past behind more completely and prove to herself once and for all that she's allowed to spend her time and energy on what she loves the most. What I'm doing now isn't repression. It's sacrifice.

I'm well aware that many people would see this as giving up too much, but they aren't the ones deciding. The idea of sacrificing my very relationship with my father is unimaginable. Unimaginable except for exactly one reason: because Charlotte needs me to.

I *do* want her happiness more than I want mine, I realize. I want it so badly that I'm willing to do whatever it takes. As I think this, the last of my reservations fall away, and the moment that follows is indescribable. In fact, there's only a single word that seems to fit. Light. Radiant, warm, bright, unquenchable light. I will honor Charlotte's choice to pick Ajay over me and allow him to be the one to help her unlock her full potential. I will let go of my jealousy and fear and step boldly into the future without fear or what comes next in my story. I will choose love over all else.

And I will let her go.

Chapter 31

Someone said once that the world will end with a whimper rather than a bang. That's how it ends up happening between me and Charlotte. We never talk about the whats or whys or wherefores. We never have a final climactic moment with a spotlight shining down on us and full orchestral score in the background. We simply drift apart. I talk to her a few more times after I make my decision, but Ajay is there half the time, and the other half she seems distracted. She doesn't mention the fact that I paid for her rent except for a quick thank you immediately afterwards.

Ajay never shows up to my disciplinary hearing, which means that I end up being expelled from school. The security cameras in the library show me clearly being the aggressor without any obvious provocation, and no one seems to buy my explanation that I thought he was trying to hurt her because I can't bring myself to tell them about Charlotte's past without her permission. I never learn why Ajay didn't show up, although I suspect that he simply got busy with other things and forgot, despite numerous reminders on my part. There's part of me that's irritated at him for it, but another part wants to just have done with this phase of my life and move on to whatever's next.

My father does indeed cut me off financially. My attempt to explain Charlotte's situation goes over exactly as well as I'd expected, which is to say that a lump of moldy bread would have had just as good a chance of getting my point across. As a result, I'm forced to move out. That's really just as well since I don't have school to worry about anymore anyway, but it still stings. My plan is to live with a distant cousin for a while as I work and save up enough money to attend the local community college where he lives. Hopefully that will give me time to find a more concrete direction for my life.

On the day I leave my apartment, both Micah and Mason are there to help me pack up and transport my belongings. As far as I know, Chris doesn't even know I'm leaving. Micah lets me use his car as I still don't have one of my own.

It's a somber atmosphere as Mason and Micah help me load up my few boxes of worldly possessions. They're both surprisingly quiet. As we wrap up, Micah hands me a twenty-dollar bill.

"Take care of yourself," he tells me.

"Mason was wrong about you," I say.

The look of surprise on his face is priceless.

"Yes, a lot of our discussions were uncomfortable, and sometimes I wished you would go bother someone else for a change, but you were also one of the only people in my life at a time that was incredibly lonely for me. So thank you," I tell him.

Mason smiles as I say this and nods in approval.

"I stand corrected."

Micah, for the second time in his life, is speechless.

"You're not a bad person, Micah," I tell him. "You're someone who is doing his best to figure out the twists and turns of life, just like the rest of us. So," my voice catches as the emotion trickles down into my voice, "I'll miss you. You take care of yourself as well."

"Okay."

I turn to Mason.

"Thank you for being there when I needed you."

He nods again.

"I try."

I lean against the door of Micah's car for a moment, letting the dying rays of the setting sun, both literal and figurative, wash over my skin. Mason's right. Some moments are not to be analyzed or logically "figured out." Some moments are just to be given permission to exist without commentary.

We stand there, the three of us, as darkness slowly descends upon us, drinking in pure experience. It's hard to tell in the low light, but for a half second I swear I see a flash of violet and a flicker of golden hair around the corner of one of the apartment buildings. If I did, I'll never know, but I like to think that Charlotte is watching from a distance, bidding a silent goodbye. Finally the moment ends, and I reach for the door to Micah's car. It's time to take this show on the road.

Chapter 32

For the next five years, I think about Charlotte. Not constantly, of course. I have plenty of other things going on in my life. I mostly wonder how she's doing, what she's been up to. I try to figure out what it all means.

It takes me multiple years to pinpoint what the miracle of it all really was. It wasn't the fact that Charlotte had such light inside of her. It was that I able to *see* that light. She *was* special, in the same-but-different way that everyone is. What was *really* special was the type of love I eventually grew to have for her.

I still love her, even now. Even though I'll never see her again. Even though I'll never tell her. It sits there, humming in the background. Rarely top of mind, but omnipresent.

In the context of my job as an agent for small-time actors, I've realized that everybody has light inside them. The problem is that many, if not most of us, have it buried so deeply that we never realize that it was ever there. For some people, like myself, the only hint that it was ever there in the first place is the emptiness, the void of meaning that subtly points toward what was there before. Others see it, but choose not to grow it, or seek only to grow it in themselves rather than in others as well.

Every once in a while I catch a glimpse of Charlotte on TV and wonder how she's doing mentally. Does she ever get panic attacks on stage? Has she been able to stay sober in an industry chock full of alcohol and drugs? I don't know, but I feel like I get a hint when she decides to take a step back from a more traditional career and focus on making music videos as a content creator.

There's a part of me that feels a little sad when I see her up on the big stage. Not because I'm not happy for her, but because there's a part of me that wishes I could still be a part of her success. But part of love is knowing when to step back, understanding and respecting another's decision to move in a different direction with their life. And trust. Trust that they will be able to overcome their demons in their own way and reach their ultimate potential.

So I sit back and watch, trying to glean clues about her emotional state from subtle glints in her violet eyes, all while continuing my own personal quest to excavate my own light.

I don't think for a moment that I've arrived, whatever that would even mean, but that's what makes it a journey, an endless hunt for that tantalizing mystery that lies just beyond the horizon. That miracle that I can never quite put into words, not even to myself, but that seems to drive the very world around us more than we know. That secret sauce that whispers the meaning of life in hints and half phrases as we struggle onward through grief and pain.

And yet, despite how bleak that all sounds, there's something about this hidden, almost unreachable love that makes it more than the sum of its parts.

The older I've gotten, the more I've found myself safeguarding my experiences with Charlotte a way similar to how she tenaciously protected her singing from those who wouldn't understand. Not crammed into a trunk in the back of the attic to collect dust, but on a pedestal in the far corner where only those who know to look for it will be able to find it. As I've done so, there's been a strange sense of distance that's developed between me and most of the rest of humanity. Not because I want it that way, but because there's no combination of words that I've been able to find that has been able to get across what exactly it is that I'm chasing.

When I say "love" they think heart flutters and kisses under the moonlight. When I say "hope" they think wishing that things would get better. When I say "faith" they think belief in a set of rules or a brick-and-mortar building.

I guess this is where this story ends. Not because it does, in fact, end here, but because it represents a natural stopping place in a voyage that will continue as long as my life does, twisting and turning in ways that I can only guess at now.

Five years to the day that I moved away from college, I step foot back onto campus for the first time. I haven't really gone out of my way to come here. It just so happens that one of my clients has an audition in this area for a small-scale musical, and I thought I may as well take a detour while I am in the area. It's a holiday, so no one's here, but fortunately for me, the buildings are still open for me to poke around in. It's surreal walking down the same sidewalks as years ago, lost in the memories. As I do so, many of the same feelings from back then come flooding in. Determination, yet lack of confidence. Pressure to perform, yet without the freedom to choose something that would make it worth it. I drink it all in like a soup, enjoying the sheer vitality of it.

Slowly I make my way to the Tanner building, where they used to have Swing Dance Club. The ballroom itself is almost just as I remember. At some point, they added a magnificent stained glass skylight in the middle of the ceiling, but the rest of it appears to be almost identical to the way it was before. I wonder if they still have club meetings here.

As I stand there, swathed in pure memory, the sun lines up with the skylight to shine a perfect beam of light onto the middle of the dance floor, almost like a natural spotlight. I step toward it, as if drawn by a magnet. How interesting that the one new feature of the place feels like the best representation of my time here.

I stand in the middle of the sunny glow, letting the warmth of the beam cascade off my shoulders. Rock step. Step. Step. Rock step. Step. Step.

The sun pours through the skylight above me, bathing myself, and all those who let it in, with irrepressible, glorious light.

THE END

About the Author

James Upsilon is a licensed mental health therapist with over five years of experience. He has been writing even longer, having finished his first novel at age 12. He is the author of The Furry Book of Nonsense, which is a chapter book for kids. He lives with his wife and three children in West Virginia.

Connect with him at jamesupsilonbooks.com

www.ingramcontent.com/pod-product-compliance
Lightning Source LLC
Chambersburg PA
CBHW020609110726
47899CB00002B/436